John Lyly's The Woman in the Moon: A Retelling

David Bruce

Published by David Bruce, 2023.

JOHN LYLY'S THE WOMAN IN THE MOON: A RETELLING

First edition. January 8, 2023.

Written by David Bruce.

Table of Contents

Dedication

Dedicated to Carl Eugene Bruce and Josephine Saturday Bruce

My father, Carl Eugene Bruce, died on 24 October 2013. He used to work for Ohio Power, and at one time, his job was to shut off the electricity of people who had not paid their bills. He sometimes would find a home with an impoverished mother and some children. Instead of shutting off their electricity, he would tell the mother that she needed to pay her bill or soon her electricity would be shut off. He would write on a form that no one was home when he stopped by because if no one was home he did not have to shut off their electricity.

The best good deed that anyone ever did for my father occurred after a storm that knocked down many power lines. He and other linemen worked long hours and got wet and cold. Their feet were freezing because water got into their boots and soaked their socks. Fortunately, a kind woman gave my father and the other linemen dry socks to wear.

My mother, Josephine Saturday Bruce, died on 14 June 2003. She used to work at a store that sold clothing. One day, an impoverished mother with a baby clothed in rags walked into the store and started shoplifting in an interesting way: The mother took the rags off her baby and dressed the infant in new clothing. My mother knew that this mother could not afford to buy the clothing, but she helped the mother dress her baby and then she watched as the

Cover Photograph for John Lyly's *The Woman in the Moon*: A Retelling:
William-Adolphe Bouguereau - Pandore
https://commons.wikimedia.org/wiki/
Category:Pandora_paintings#/media/
File:William-Adolphe_Bouguereau_-_Pandore.jpg

***

This is a short, quick, and easy read.

Anecdotes are usually short humorous stories. Sometimes they are thought-provoking or informative, not amusing.

***

Educate Yourself
Read Like A Wolf Eats
Be Excellent to Each Other
Books Then, Books Now, Books Forever

***

In this retelling, as in all my retellings, I have tried to make the work of literature accessible to modern readers who may lack some of the knowledge about mythology, religion, and history that the literary work's contemporary audience had.

Do you know a language other than English? If you do, I give you permission to translate this book, copyright your translation, publish or self-publish it, and keep all the royalties for yourself. (Do give me credit, of course, for the original retelling.)

I would like to see my retellings of classic literature used in schools, so I give permission to the country of Finland (and all other countries) to get an eBook copy of this book and give copies to all students forever. I also give permission to the state of Texas (and all other states) to get an eBook copy of this book and give copies to all students forever. I also give permission to all teachers to get an eBook copy of this book and give copies to all students forever.

Teachers need not actually teach my retellings. Teachers are welcome to give students copies of my eBooks as background material. For example, if they are teaching Homer's *Iliad* and *Odyssey*, teachers are welcome to give students copies of my *Virgil's* Aeneid: *A Retelling in Prose* and tell students, "Here's another ancient epic you may want to read in your spare time."

CAST OF CHARACTERS

Nature. Nature is the main deity in this play. In Greek and Roman mythology, Jupiter (Greek name: Zeus) was the King of the gods. But in this play, Nature is a greater deity than Jupiter.

Concord, handmaid of Nature.

Discord, handmaid of Nature.

Note: Concord and Discord are both the handmaids of Nature because, as Nature says early in the play, "Nature works her will from contraries."

Saturn, one of the seven planets. Saturn is associated with melancholy.

Jupiter, one of the seven planets. Jupiter is associated with power.

Mars, one of the seven planets. Mars is associated with war and fighting.

Sol, one of the seven planets. Sol — the Sun — is associated with wisdom.

Venus, one of the seven planets. Venus is associated with love.

Mercury, one of the seven planets. Mercury is associated with trickery and eloquence.

Luna, one of the seven planets. Luna is the Moon, which is associated with change

Note: John Lyly's society believed that there were seven planets, including the Sun (Sol), which they called a planet. His society believed that the planets were embedded in crystalline spheres that orbited the Earth, which was the center of the universe.

Juno, Jupiter's jealous wife.

Ganymede, attendant on Jupiter. Ganymede is a mute character: He has no lines.

Cupid, son of Venus.

Joculus, son of Venus.

Pandora, the woman in the moon. She is the first woman. Nature creates her after Nature previously created men.

Stesias, Utopian shepherd.

Learchus, Utopian shepherd.

Melos, Utopian shepherd.

Iphicles, Utopian shepherd.

Gunophilus, loyal servant to Pandora.

SCENE:

Utopia. Etymologically, "Utopia" means "no place." In this play, Utopia is located on Earth, and the goddess Nature has her workshop there.

NOTES:

This is the only play that John Lyly wrote as poetry: It is blank verse. His other plays were written in prose. David Bruce's retelling is in prose.

In this society, a person of higher rank would use "thou," "thee," "thine," and "thy" when referring to a person of lower rank. (These terms were also used affectionately and between equals.) A person of lower rank would use "you" and "your" when referring to a person of higher rank.

The word "wench" at this time was not necessarily negative. It was often used affectionately.

The word "mistress" at this time can mean simply a woman who is loved. It can also mean a female head of household.

The word "fair" can mean attractive, beautiful, handsome, and good-looking.

COSMOLOGY:

According to John Lyly's society, the planet Earth is composed of four elements. The element earth is at the center. Water covers the earth, with the continents and islands being bits of earth poking out of the water. Above the water is air. Above the air is a sphere of fire that separates the Earth from the Moon. (The sphere of fire was controversial: After people began to believe in the heliocentric theory, people began to stop believing in the sphere of fire.)

According to John Lyly's society, the Earth is composed of parts that make up one whole. Also according to John Lyly's society, the same is true of the universe.

At the center of the universe is the Earth, then comes the sphere of fire, and then come nine other spheres: the seven spheres of seven planets, the sphere of the firmament, and then (according to Christians) the Empyreal Heaven. The firmament is where the constellations and fixed stars are embedded. (Mercury, Venus, Mars, Jupiter, and Saturn are called "wandering stars" or "erring stars" because they wander in the sky; the word "planet" comes from a Greek term and means "wandering star." One meaning of "err" is "wander.") Furthest away from the Earth is Heaven.

The seven planets, in order of distance from the centric Earth, are the Moon, Mercury, Venus, Sun, Mars, Jupiter, and Saturn. Yes, this culture called the Sun a planet.

HUMORS AND ELEMENTS:

This society believed that the mixture of four humors in the body determined one's temperament. One humor could be predominant. The four humors are blood, yellow bile, black bile, and phlegm.

If blood is predominant, then the person is sanguine (active, optimistic).

If yellow bile is predominant, then the person is choleric (bad-tempered).

If black bile is predominant, then the person is melancholic (sad).

If phlegm is predominant, then the person is phlegmatic (calm, apathetic, indolent).

Humors could be hot, cold, wet, or dry.

Blood is hot and wet.

Yellow bile is hot and dry.

Black bile is cold and dry.

Phlegm is cold and wet.

This society also believed that everything was created out of four elements: fire, air, water, and earth. These were associated with the four humors.

Fire was represented by yellow bile.

Air was represented by blood.

Water was represented by phlegm.

Earth was represented by black bile.

EDITIONS:

Lyly, John. *The Complete Plays of John Lyly*. Edited by R. Warwick Bond. Oxford: At the Clarendon Press, 1973.

Lyly, John. *The Woman in the Moon*. Ed. Leah Scragg. The Revels Plays. Manchester and New York: Manchester University Press, 2006.

Lyly, John. *The Plays of John Lyly*. Carter A. Daniel, editor. Lewisburg: Bucknell University Press. London and Toronto: Associated University Presses, 1988.

PROLOGUE

The Prologue said to you, the readers:

"Our Poet slumbering in the Muses' laps,

"Has seen a woman seated in the Moon,

"A point beyond the ancient theoric."

The ancient theoric is the old belief. In this case, it is the belief in the man in the Moon. John Lyly is going beyond the old belief and introducing the woman in the Moon.

"And as it was, so he presents his dream,

"Here in the bounds of fair Utopia,

"Where lonely Nature being [the] only Queen,

"Bestows such workmanship on earthly mold [form]

"That [the] Heavens themselves envy her glorious work.

"But all in vain; for, malice being spent,

"They yield themselves to follow Nature's doom [judgment].

"And fair Pandora sits in Cynthia's orb."

Cynthia is the goddess of the Moon. She is a tripartite goddess. On Earth, she is known as Diana. In the Underworld, she is known as Hecate. In the Heavens, she is known as Cynthia and as Luna.

The Prologue continued:

"This, but [just] the shadow of our author's dream,

"Argues the substance to be near at hand:

"At whose appearance I most humbly crave,

"That in your forehead she may read content.

"If many faults escape in her discourse,

"Remember all is but [only] a poet's dream,

"The first he had in Phoebus' holy bower."

Phoebus Apollo is the god of poetry and many other things.

The Prologue continued:

"But not the last — unless the first displease."

CHAPTER 1

— 1.1 —

Nature and her two handmaidens, Concord and Discord, stood in Nature's workshop, which was located on Earth.

Nature said to Concord and Discord:

"Nature descends from far above the spheres of the seven planets to frolic here in fair Utopia, where my chief works flourish in their prime, and frolic in their first simplicity and innocence.

"Here I survey the pictured firmament."

In her workshop, Nature had a model of the universe. The universe was filled with the four elements: fire, air, water, and earth. John Lyly's society believed that everything in the universe was created from these four elements.

As Nature mentioned various parts of her model of the universe, she pointed to them.

Nature continued:

"Hurtless flames are found in the arch of the Moon."

Just below the sphere of the Moon was a Sphere of Fire. The flames that Nature was referring to are hurtless because they are not real: They are a part of a work of art. A sphere that is partially above the horizon forms an arch.

Nature continued:

"Here is the liquid substance of the welkin's waste, where moisture's treasury is clouded up."

The welkin is the sky, which stores much water in the form of clouds. "Waste" means "untouched area."

Nature continued:

"Here is the mutual jointure and conjunction of all swelling seas and all the creatures which their waves contain.

"Lastly is the rundle — that is, the globe — of this massive earth, from utmost face to the center's point."

The utmost face was the place on Earth furthest from the center of the Earth.

Nature continued:

"All these, and all their endless circumstance — everything that appertains to them — I survey here, and I glory in myself.

"But why does Discord so knit her brows, with sorrow's cloud eclipsing our delights?"

Discord said:

"It grieves my heart that always in every work, my fellow Concord frustrates my desires.

"When I, to perfect some wondrous deed, bring forth good and bad, or light and dark, pleasant and sad, moving and fixed things, frail and immortal, or like contraries, Concord with her hand unites them all in one, and so makes void and nullified the end of my attempt."

Nature said:

"I tell thee, Discord, while you twain attend on Nature's train, your work must prove to be but one, and although in yourselves you are different, yet in my service you must agree well.

"For Nature works her will from contraries."

Nature works from the use of Concord and Discord. Think of the yin yang symbol in Chinese philosophy. Yin and yang are two opposite but interconnected forces. The yin yang symbol has two sections, with a part of each force in each section.

Many religions believe that an orderly universe was created from chaos.

Nature looked up and said:

"But see where our Utopian shepherds come."

The four Utopian shepherds — Stesias, Learchus, Melos, and Iphicles — all clad in animal skins, entered the scene and knelt before Nature.

"Thou sovereign Queen and Author of the world, of all that was, or is, or shall be framed and made, to finish up the heap of thy great gifts, grant thy simple servants' one request," Stesias said.

"Stand up and tell me the sum of your desire," Nature said. "The boon would be great that Nature would not grant. It always was and always shall be my joy, with wholesome gifts to bless my workmanship."

Iphicles said:

"We crave, fair goddess, at thy Heavenly hands, to have as every other creature has, a sure and certain means among ourselves to propagate the issue of our kind.

"As it would be comfort to our sole estate, so it would be ease to thy working hand."

The shepherds stood up.

The shepherds wanted a way to have children. If Nature were to make women, the shepherds could have children. That would bring the shepherds comfort, and it would make Nature's work easier because she would not have to keep on creating men.

Iphicles continued:

"Each fish that swims in the floating sea, each winged fowl that soars in the air, and every beast that feeds on the ground have mates of pleasure to uphold their brood and create children.

"But thy Utopians, poor and simple men, still bewail their lack of the female sex."

Nature said:

"A female you shall have, my lovely swains, like yourselves, but of a purer mold. Meanwhile, go away from here, and tend your tender flocks, and when I send her to you, see that you consider her dear."

A swain is 1) a shepherd, and/or 2) a lover.

The shepherds exited, singing a roundelay — a short, simple song — in praise of Nature.

Nature then said to Concord and Discord:

"Now, virgins, put your hands to holy work, so that we may frame new wonders and present them to the world."

Concord and Discord drew the curtains from before Nature's workshop, where stood a clothed image and some unclothed images. They brought forth the clothed image, which resembled a statue.

Nature said:

"When I arrayed and dressed this lifeless image thus, it was decreed in my deep providence to make it such as our Utopians crave, a mirror of the Earth, and the Heavens' envy."

She wanted to create the first woman and have it be a model — an example — worthy of admiration, although she knew that doing so would make the Heavenly bodies — the seven planets — envious.

Nature continued:

"The matter first when it was void of form, was purest water, and earth, and air, and fire, and when I shaped it in a matchless mold, whereof the like was never seen before, it grew to this impression that you see, and lacks nothing now but life and soul."

Nature had made the image out of the purest elements.

Nature continued:

"But life and soul I shall inspire from Heaven, so hold it fast, until with my quickening — my life-giving — breath, I kindle inward seeds of sense and mind."

Nature's breath would give the image life and soul.

Nature continued:

"Now fire be turned to choler, air to blood, water to humor purer than itself, and earth to flesh clearer than crystal rock."

Nature was making the first woman out of the four elements: fire, air, water, and earth. Nature was also making the first woman out of a mixture of humors.

This society believed that the mixture of four humors in the body determined one's temperament. One humor could be predominant. The four humors are blood, yellow bile, black bile, and phlegm.

The humor represented by air is blood.

The humor represented by fire is yellow bile.

The humor represented by earth is black bile.

The humor represented by water is phlegm.

Nature continued:

"And Discord stand aloof, so that Concord's hands may join the spirit with the flesh in league."

Concord closely embraced the image.

She said, "Now I feel how life and inward sense imparts motion to every limb."

Nature said:

"Then let her stand or move or walk alone."

The image walked about fearfully.

"Fearfully" can mean that the image was afraid or that she made those watching her — the audience — feel fear.

Nature continued:

"Herein has Nature gone beyond herself, and Heaven will grudge and complain at the beauty of the Earth, when it spies a second Sun below."

Discord said, "Now every part performs her function's due, except the tongue whose strings are still united — still tied."

Nature said, "Discord, unloosen her tongue, to serve her turn, for in distress that must be her defense, and from that root will many mischiefs grow, if once she stains her state of innocence."

The image knelt and said to Nature, "Hail, Heavenly Queen, the Author of all good, whose will has wrought in me the fruits of life, and whose will has filled me with an understanding soul to know the difference between good and bad."

Nature helped her stand up and said:

"I make thee to be a solace to men. See that thou follow our commanding will.

"Now are thou Nature's glory and delight, compact of every Heavenly excellence.

"Thou are endowed with Saturn's deep conceit and power of thought.

"Thy mind is as haute — as elevated — as Jupiter's high thoughts.

"Thy stomach — your temperament and courage — is lion-like, like the heart of Mars, god of war.

"Thine eyes are bright beamed, like Sol — the Sun — in his array.

"Thy cheeks are more beautiful than fair Venus' cheeks.

"Thy tongue is more eloquent than Mercury's."

Among other things, Mercury was the god of eloquence.

Nature continued:

"Thy forehead is whiter than the silver Moon's.

"Thus have I robbed the planets for thy sake.

"Besides all this, thou have proud Juno's arms,

"Aurora's hands, and lovely Thetis' foot."

Juno is the wife of Jupiter. Aurora is the goddess of the dawn. Thetis is a sea goddess who is the mother of Achilles, the greatest warrior of the Trojan War.

Nature continued:

"Use all these gifts well, and Nature is thy friend, but use them ill, and Nature is thy foe.

"Now, so that thy name may suit thy qualities, I give to thee 'Pandora' for thy name."

The name "Pandora" means "many-gifted."

The seven planets entered the scene and looked at Pandora, who sat quietly.

Noticing that Pandora had some of their best attributes, the seven planets were unhappy.

"What creature have we here? A newfound gaud and plaything?" Saturn asked. "A second man, less perfect than the first?"

"Less perfect than the first" man? No. Nature created Pandora to be more perfect than the first man.

Saturn and the other planets spoke contemptuously and sarcastically to and about Pandora.

"A woman this is, indeed, but she was made in haste, to rob us planets of our ornaments," Mars said.

"Is this the saint who steals my Juno's arms?" Jupiter said.

Juno was renowned for the beauty of her arms, but Pandora's arms were more beautiful.

"My eyes?" Sol said. "Then govern thou my daylight car."

Sol is the Sun. The daylight car is the chariot that the Sun-god drives across the sky each day to bring light and heat to the Earth.

"My cheeks?" Venus said. "Then Cupid be at thy command."

Cupid was the son of Venus, but he frequently disobeyed her.

"My tongue?" Mercury said. "Thou pretty parrot, speak a while."

Parrots speak without understanding what they are saying.

"My forehead?" Luna said. "Then fair 'Cynthia,' shine by night."

Cynthia is the Moon-goddess. "Luna" and "Cynthia" are different names for the same goddess.

Luna was calling Pandora "Cynthia" sarcastically.

Nature said:

"What foul contempt is this you planets use against the glory of my words and work?

"It was my will, and that shall stand for law, and she is framed — created — to darken all your prides. Didn't I ordain your motions, and yourselves? And do you dare to check and rebuke the author of your lives? Weren't your lights contrived in Nature's workshop?

"But I have the means to end what I have begun and to make Death triumph in your lives' decay.

"If thus you cross the meed of my deserts — resist giving me what I deserve — and interfere with what I have created, be sure that I will dissolve your harmony, when once you touch the fixed period of your sway."

Nature created the harmony of the universe, and if she wished, she could change that harmony into disharmony.

Nature continued:

"Meanwhile, I leave my worthy workmanship here to obscure and dim the pride of your disdain."

Nature exited.

Despite Nature's threat, the seven planets rebelled against her.

Saturn said:

"Then in revenge of Nature and her work, let us conclude to show our empery — our power. Let us agree to bend our forces against this earthly star who is named Pandora.

"Each one in turn shall signorize — that is, rule — for a while, so that Pandora may feel the influence of our beams, and rue that she was formed in our despite — in scorn of us."

This society believed that the planets influenced human personality and events, and it believed that beams emanated from the planets.

Saturn continued:

"My turn is first, and I, Saturn, will begin."

He — Saturn — ascended.

In the theater, Saturn ascended to the balcony that was part of the stage.

Jupiter said:

"And I'll begin where Saturn makes an end, and when I end, then Mars shall tyrannize, and after Mars then Sol shall marshal — that is, govern — her, and after Sol each other planet shall tyrannize in his turn.

The other planets, in turn, were Venus, Mercury, and the Moon. Because Venus and the Moon have goddesses, Jupiter should have said "his or her," not "his."

"Come, let us go, so that Saturn may begin."

All the planets except Saturn exited.

Saturn said:

"By corrupting her purest blood, I shall instill such a melancholy mood that shall first with sullen sorrows cloud her brain, and then surround her heart with froward — that is, perverse — worry and concern.

"She shall be sick with passions of the heart, self-willed, and tongue-tied and incapable of speech, but full fraught with tears."

All of the planets were going to change Pandora's personality. Saturn was going to make her melancholic.

Gunophilus entered the scene.

He said:

"Gracious Pandora, Nature, thy good friend, has sent me, Gunophilus, to wait on thee and be thy servant.

"Because obedience is the proper response to Nature's will, and because of the graces of thy lovely self, Gunophilus will serve thee humbly, and he is resolved to live and die with thee."

"If Nature willed this, then attend on me, but little service have I to command," Pandora said. "If I myself might choose my kind of life, neither thou nor anyone else would stay with me. I find myself unfit for company."

"Why is that, fair mistress in your flowering youth, when pleasure's joy should sit in every thought of yours?" Gunophilus asked.

Pandora was already afflicted with melancholy by Saturn. A melancholic person is sad, gloomy, sullen, brooding, and often irritable.

Pandora said:

"Avaunt, sir sauce! Go away, saucy boy! Do you play the questioner?

"What is it to thee whether I am sick or sad?

"Either conduct thyself in a better way or get thee away from here and serve some other where."

Gunophilus said to himself, "This is a sour beginning, but there is no remedy. Nature has bound me to serve Pandora, and I must obey. I see that servants must have merchants' ears, to bear the blast and brunt of every wind."

Servants and merchants must put up with rude bosses and with rude customers.

Pandora said:

"What throbs are these that labor in my breast? What swelling clouds are these that overcast my brain?

"I burst, unless by tears they turn to rain. I grudge and grieve, but I do not know well why. And I choose to weep rather than speak my mind, for fretful sorrow captivates my tongue."

Pandora was both rude and sad, without knowing why.

She played the vixen with everything about her; that is, she vented her anger on everything around her. Finally, she resumed her seat.

The four Utopian shepherds — Stesias, Iphicles, Melos, and Learchus — entered the scene.

Looking at Pandora, Stesias said:

"See where she sits, she in whom we must delight.

"Beware! She sleeps. Make no noise for fear of waking her!"

"She is asleep?" Iphicles said. "Why, see how her alluring eyes with open looks do glance on every side."

"O eyes fairer than is the morning star!" Melos said.

"Nature herself is not so lovely fair!" Learchus said.

Stesias said:

"Let us with reverence kiss her lily-white hands —"

They all knelt before her.

Stesias added:

"— and by deserts in service to her win her love."

He then said to Pandora:

"Sweet Dame, if Stesias may content thine eye, command my neat, my flock, and my tender kids, of which a great store overspread our plains."

"Neat" are cattle, and "kids" are young goats.

Stesias then said:

"Allow me, sweet mistress, just to kiss thy hand."

Pandora hit him on the lips.

Part of being melancholic is being easy to anger.

Stesias stood up.

Learchus said:

"No, Stesias, no. Learchus is the man for her."

He said to Pandora:

"Thou mirror of Dame Nature's cunning, skillful work, let me just hold thee by that sacred hand, and I shall make thee our Utopian queen, and set a gilded chaplet on thy head, so that nymphs and satyrs may admire thy pomp."

A chaplet is an ornamental wreath.

Pandora hit his hand. Learchus stood up.

Gunophilus said to himself, "These twain and I have fortunes all alike."

All three of them had endured Pandora's anger.

Melos said, "Sweet Nature's pride, let me just see thy hand, and servant like, Melos shall wait on thee, and carry the train of thy dress, just as in the glorious Heavens, Perseus supports his love — Andromeda — whose thirty stars, whether they rise or fall, Perseus falls or rises, hanging at her heels."

Andromeda was a maiden who was chained to a rock to be a sacrifice to a sea-monster. The hero Perseus rescued her, and then he married her. Their constellations are close together in the sky, and Perseus still serves his loved one.

Pandora thrust her hands in her pockets so that Melos could not see them. Melos stood up.

Iphicles said, "Then to bless the love of Iphicles, whose heart regards thee as dearer than himself, just behold me with a loving look, and I will lead thee in our solemn dance, teaching thee tunes, and pleasant lays — songs — of love."

Many shepherds are musicians.

Pandora closed her eyes and frowned. Iphicles stood up.

Stesias said:

"No kiss? No touch? No friendly look?

"What churlish influence deprives her mind? For Nature said that she was innocent, and fully fraught — fully filled — with virtuous qualities."

Of course, Pandora was under the malignant influence of Saturn.

Stesias said to Pandora:

"But speak, sweet love. Thou cannot speak but well."

Gunophilus said, "She is not tongue tied. I know that by the proof of experience."

He had experienced Pandora's sharp tongue.

"Speak once, Pandora, to thy loving friends," Melos requested.

"Rude knaves, what do you mean thus to trouble me?" Pandora asked.

Gunophilus said, "She spoke to you, my masters. I am not one of your company."

Pandora sank to the ground and wept.

Learchus said:

"Alas! Weeping, she swoons.

"Gunophilus, help to raise thy mistress from the ground."

"This is the very passion of the heart, and melancholy is the ground thereof," Gunophilus said.

Stesias said:

"Then to sift that humor from her heart, let us with roundelays — with songs — delight her ear, for I have heard that music is a means to calm the rage of melancholy mood."

The four shepherds and Gunophilus sang.

Pandora stood up and ran away at the end of the song, saying:

"What songs? What pipes? And what fiddling have we here?

"Won't you allow me to take my rest?"

She exited.

Melos said:

"What shall we do to vanquish her disease — her vexation? The death of that vexation would be life to our desires.

"But let us go and follow her. We must not leave her like this."

The four shepherds and Gunophilus exited.

Saturn descended on the stage.

Alone, Saturn said:

"Saturn has laid the foundation for the rest of the planets, on which they can build the ruin of this dame, and spot and spoil her innocence with vicious thoughts.

"My turn has passed, and Jupiter's turn is next."

Saturn exited.

CHAPTER 2

— 2.1 —

Accompanied by Ganymede, Jupiter, who was holding a golden scepter, said to himself:

"*A Jove principium, sunt et Jovis omnia plena.*"

The Latin means: From Jove everything gets its beginning, and with Jove everything is filled.

Jove is another name for Jupiter.

Jupiter continued talking to himself:

"Now Jupiter shall rule Pandora's thoughts and fill her with ambition and disdain. I will enforce my influence to the worst, lest the other planets blame my rule over her for being lenient."

As King of the gods, Jupiter knew about ambition and disdain. He ruled the other gods by might.

Jupiter ascended.

In the theater, Jupiter ascended to the balcony that was part of the stage.

Pandora and Gunophilus entered the scene.

Pandora's melancholy had passed, but now she was afflicted with ambition and disdain by Jupiter.

Pandora said:

"Although rancor now has been rooted from my heart, I feel it burdened in another way.

"By day I think of nothing but of rule. By night my dreams are all of empery: absolute power.

"My ears delight to hear of sovereignty.

"My tongue desires to speak of princely sway.

"My eye wishes that every object were a crown."

Jupiter said to himself:

"Danae was fair, and Leda pleased me well, lovely Callisto set my heart on fire, and in my eye Europa was a gem."

Disguised as a shower of gold, Jupiter slept with Danae, who bore him a son: the hero Perseus.

Disguised as a swan, Jupiter seduced Leda, who bore him two daughters: Helen, who later became known as Helen of Troy, and Clytemnestra, who married and later murdered Agamemnon, leader of the Greek forces against the Trojans.

Disguised as Diana, Jupiter was able to be close to Callisto, a follower of the goddess Diana, goddess of the hunt. When she was separated from her friends, he raped her. Juno, who hated the women whom her husband slept with, even when they were raped, turned Callisto into a bear. Years later, Callisto saw her son, Arcas, who prepared to defend himself with a spear against what he thought was a bear. Jupiter turned Arcas and Callisto into constellations. Callisto became Ursa Major: Big Bear. Arcas became Ursa Minor: Little Bear.

Disguised as a bull, Jupiter kidnapped the Phoenician woman Europa, who climbed on his back. He then swam to Crete, where Europa bore him a son: King Midas.

Jupiter continued:

"But in the beauty of this paragon, Pandora, Dame Nature has gone far beyond herself, and in this one are all my loves contained, and come what can come, Jupiter shall test whether fair Pandora will accept his love.

"But first I must dismiss this Heavenly cloud that hides me from the sight of mortal eyes."

The gods were able to hide themselves with a cloud from mortals.

Jupiter waved away the cloud and said:

"Behold, Pandora, where thy lover sits, high Jove himself, who ravished with thy blaze and glory, receives more influence than he pours on thee, and humbly sues for succor at thy hands."

The kind of succor he wanted was an orgasm.

"Why, who are thou more than Utopian swains?" Pandora asked.

Jupiter said, "I am King of the gods, I am one of immortal race, and I am he who with a beck — a gesture — controls the Heavens."

"Why, then Pandora does exceed the Heavens — Pandora neither fears nor loves Jupiter," Pandora said.

Jupiter said:

"Thy beauty will excuse whatever thou say, and in thy looks thy words are privileged.

"But if Pandora understood those gifts that Jove can give, she would esteem his love, for I can make thee Empress of the world, and seat thee in the glorious firmament."

Some of Jupiter's lovers became constellations.

Pandora said:

"The words 'Empress' and 'firmament' please my ears more than Jupiter pleases my eyes.

"Yet if thy love is like the words you have said, give me thy golden scepter in my hand. But do not give it to me as purchase price of my precious love, for that is more than Heaven itself is worth."

Jupiter tossed her the golden scepter and said, "There, hold the scepter of eternal Jove, but do not let majesty increase thy pride."

Pandora said, "What do I lack now except an imperial throne and Ariadne's starlight diadem?"

Ariadne helped Theseus defeat the half-bull, half-human Minotaur on the island of Crete. She sailed away with Theseus, but he abandoned her on the island of Naxos. The god Bacchus found her, married her, and gave her a crown composed of stars.

Juno, Jupiter's jealous (for good reason) wife, entered the scene.

Angry, she said:

"False, perjured Jupiter, and full of guile, are these the fruits of thy new government?

"Are Juno's beauty and thy wedlock vow and all my kindness trodden under foot? Wasn't it enough to fancy such a trull — such a prostitute — but thou must yield thy scepter to her hand?

"I thought that Ganymede had weaned thy heart from the lawless lust of any woman's love. But I see well that every time thou stray, thy lust only looks for strumpet stars below."

Ganymede was a beautiful boy whom Jupiter, disguised as an eagle, had kidnapped to be his cupbearer — and, according to some sources, his lover. The Latin form of "Ganymede" is *Catamitus*. A catamite is a boy kept for homosexual purposes.

Pandora said to Juno, "Why, know that Pandora scorns both Jove and thee, and there she lays his scepter on the ground."

Pandora put the golden scepter on the ground, and Juno picked it up.

Holding the golden scepter, Juno said:

"This shall go with me to our Celestial court, where the gods shall see thy shame, fond, foolish Jupiter, and laugh at Love for tainting majesty."

Love is Cupid, the son of Venus. Cupid shoots golden arrows that cause people and gods to fall in love.

Juno continued:

"And when you please, you will come to us."

She then said to Pandora:

"But as for thee, thou shameless counterfeit, thy pride shall quickly lose her painted plumes and feel the heavy weight of Juno's wrath."

Juno exited.

Pandora said:

"Let Juno fret, and move the powers of Heaven, yet Pandora stands secure in herself.

"Aren't I Nature's darling and her pride? Hasn't she spent her treasure all on me?"

Jupiter said, "Yet be thou wise (I counsel thee for love) and fear displeasure at a goddess' hand."

Juno sometimes did horrible things to the women her husband slept with.

For example, a mortal woman named Semele had sex with Jupiter, King of the gods, after making him swear an inviolable oath that he would grant her whatever she wished for. After Jupiter and Semele had slept together, Juno convinced Semele to ask Jupiter to reveal himself to her in his true form although Juno knew what would happen to Semele. Having sworn an inviolable oath, Jupiter had to grant the wish, but seeing Jupiter in his true form was too much for Semele, and she died. She was carrying a fetus, which Jupiter rescued and sewed into his thigh. Jupiter later gave birth to Bacchus, the god of wine and ecstasy.

"I tell thee, Jupiter, Pandora's worth is far exceeding the worth of all your goddesses," Pandora said. "And since in her — Juno — thou obscure and diminish my praise, here, to be short, I abjure thy love."

Jupiter said:

"I may not blame thee, for my beams are the cause of all this insolence and proud disdain. But to prevent a second raging storm if jealous Juno should by chance return, here ends my love.

"Pandora, now farewell."

Jupiter wrapped himself and Ganymede in a cloud and exited skyward.

Pandora said:

"And are thou clouded up? Fare as thou list: Do as thou wish. Pandora's heart shall never stoop to Jove."

She then said to her servant:

"Gunophilus, base vassal as thou are, how did it happen that when Juno was in presence here, thou did not honor me with kneel and crouch, and lay thy hands under my precious foot —"

Placing one's hands under the feet of another person was a sign of submission.

Gunophilus bowed repeatedly.

Pandora continued:

"— to make her know the height of my deserving?

"Base peasant, humbly watch my stately looks, and yield applause to every word I speak, or from my service I'll discard thee quite."

On his knees, Gunophilus said:

"Fair and dread sovereign! Lady of the world!

"Even then when jealous Juno was in place, as I beheld the glory of thy face, my feeble eyes, admiring thy majesty, there did sink into my heart such holy fear — that very fear amazing and bewildering every sense of mine — that I withheld my tongue from saying what I would, and that fear froze my joints from bowing when they should."

Pandora said, "Aye, Gunophilus, now thou please me. These words and curtsies — bows — prove that thou are dutiful."

The four Utopian shepherds — Stesias, Iphicles, Melos, and Learchus — entered the scene.

"Now, Stesias, speak," Stesias said.

"Learchus, plead for love," Learchus said.

Iphicles said, "Now, Cyprian Queen, guider of loving thoughts, help Iphicles."

The Cyprian Queen is Venus, the sexually active goddess of sexual passion, who was born off the shore of the island of Cyprus.

"Melos must speed — that is, succeed — or die," Melos said.

Gunophilus, stepping between the shepherds and Pandora, said, "Where are you going, now, my masters, in such posthaste? Her excellence is not at leisure now."

In this context, "masters" means "sirs."

Of course, they were going to court Pandora.

"Sweet Gunophilus, further our attempts," Stesias said.

"And we shall make thee rich with our rewards," Iphicles said.

"Stay here until I know her further pleasure," Gunophilus said.

He turned to Pandora and said, "Stesias and his fellows humbly crave access to your excellence."

"Aye, now thou fit my humor — my mood," Pandora said. "Let them come."

"Come on, masters," Gunophilus said.

The shepherds approached Pandora and spoke to her.

"Tell me, my dear, when comes that happy hour, whereon thy love shall guerdon — shall reward — my desire," Stesias asked.

"How long shall sorrow's winter pinch my heart, and how long shall my lukewarm hopes be chilled with freezing fear, before my suit obtains thy sweet consent?" Learchus asked.

Iphicles asked, "How long shall death, encroaching by delays, abridge the course of my decaying life before Pandora loves poor Iphicles?"

"How long shall cares cut off my flowering prime, before the harvest of my love shall be in?" Melos asked.

Stesias requested, "Speak, sweet love!"

"Speak some gentle words, sweet love," Iphicles requested.

"Let thy tongue first salve Learchus' wound that first was made with those immortal eyes," Learchus said.

Melos said, "The only — the mere — promise of thy future love will drown the secret heaps of my despair in an endless ocean of expected joys."

Pandora said, "Although my breast has yet never harbored love, yet my bounty and generosity would free you from your servitude, if love might well consort with and accompany our majesty and not debase our matchless dignity."

Pandora was using the royal plural when she said the phrase "our matchless dignity."

"Sweet honey words, but sauced with bitter gall," Stesias said.

"They draw me on, and yet they put me back," Iphicles said.

"They hold me up, and yet they let me fall," Learchus said.

"They give me life, and yet they let me die," Melos said.

"But as thou will, so give me sweet or sour, for in thy pleasure must be my content and happiness," Stesias said.

"Whether thou draw me on, or put me back, I must admire thy beauty's wildness," Iphicles said.

"And as thou will, so let me stand or fall," Learchus said. "Love has decreed thy word must govern me."

"And as thou will, so let me live or die," Melos said. "In life or death, I must obey thy will."

Pandora said:

"I please myself in your humility, yet I will make some test and trial of your faith, before I stoop to favor your laments, for you know well that Pandora knows her worth.

"He who will purchase — that is, win — things of greatest prize, must conquer by his deeds, and not by his words.

"Go then, all four of you, and slay the savage boar, which roving up and down with ceaseless rage, destroys the fruit of our Utopian fields, and he who first presents me with his head shall wear my glove in favor of the deed."

The gift of a glove by a woman honored the man who received it. The man would wear the glove on his hat.

"We go, Pandora," Melos said.

"Nay, we run!" Learchus said.

"We fly!" Stesias said.

The shepherds exited.

Pandora said to herself:

"Thus must Pandora exercise these swains, commanding them to do dangerous exploits, and even if they were kings, my beauty would still command them."

She then said:

"Sirrah Gunophilus, hold up the train of my dress."

Pandora and Gunophilus exited.

— 2.2 —

Alone, Mars said to himself:

"Mars comes entreated by Juno, the Queen of Heaven, to summon Jove from this his regiment: his period of rulership over Pandora.

"Such a jealous humor — a jealous mood — crows and cries out in her brain that she is mad until he returns from here."

He then said loudly so that Jupiter would hear him:

"Now, Sovereign Jove, King of immortal kings, thy lovely Juno long has expected thee, and until thou come, she thinks that every hour is a year."

Jupiter removed the cloud hiding Ganymede and him, and then they came down from above.

Jupiter said:

"And Jove will go the sooner to assuage and sooth her frantic, idle, and suspicious thoughts, for I know well that Pandora troubles Juno, nor will Juno calm the tempest of her mind until with a whirlwind of outrageous words, she beats my ears, and weeps her curst — her shrewish — heart away."

Crying will make Juno feel better.

Jupiter continued:

"Yet I will go, for words are just a blast of wind, and sunshine will ensue when storms are past.

Jupiter and Ganymede exited.

Mars ascended.

Mars, in his seat, said:

"Now bloody Mars begins to play his part. I'll work such war within Pandora's breast, and somewhat more because of Juno's fair request that after all her churlishness and pride, she shall become a vixen martialist."

Pandora shall now become a woman warrior.

The four Utopian shepherds returned with the boar's head. Stesias was carrying a spear.

"Here let us stay until fair Pandora comes, and then Stesias shall have his due reward," Stesias said.

"And why not Iphicles as well as you?" Iphicles askedd.

"The prize is mine," Minos said. "My sword cut off his head."

"But first my spear wounded him to the death," Learchus said.

"He did not fall down until I had gored his side," Stesias said.

"Be content, all of you, Learchus did the deed, and I will make it good, whoever says nay," Learchus said.

He would fight anyone who opposed his claim to have killed the boar.

"Melos will die before he loses his right," Melos said.

Iphicles said:

"Nay, then it is time to snatch the head."

He grabbed the boar's head and said:

"The head is mine."

"Lay the boar's head down, or I shall lay thee on the earth," Stesias said.

They fought.

Pandora and Gunophilus entered the scene.

Pandora said:

"Aye, so I see how it is: fair and far off, for fear of being hurt. See how the cowards counterfeit a fight."

A fair distance is a cordial distance.

Pandora continued:

"Strike home, you dastard swains, strike home, I say!"

"Strike home" means "deliver a death blow."

Pandora continued:

"Do you fight in jest? Let me bestir myself then and see if I can cudgel all four of you."

She snatched the spear out of Stesias' hand and lay around her, fighting all four shepherds at once.

Gunophilus said, "What! Is my mistress now masculine mankind all of a sudden?"

"Alas!" Learchus said. "Why does Pandora strike her best friends?"

A "friend" is a male admirer.

Pandora said:

"My friends? Base peasants! My friends would fight like men.

"Avaunt! Get out, or I shall lay you all out for dead."

The shepherds, except Stesias, exited.

Stesias said to Pandora:

"See, cruel fair, how thou have wronged thy friend."

He showed her his shirt, which was all bloody.

Stesias continued:

"Thou spill the blood of him who kept it just for thee.

"There's my desert."

He pointed to the boar's head on the ground. He believed that he deserved a reward for killing the boar.

Stesias continued:

"And here is my reward."

He pointed to his wound.

Stesias continued:

"I dare not say this from an ingrateful and ungrateful mind, but if Pandora had been well advised, I dare to say that Stesias would have been spared."

"Begone, I say, before I strike again," Pandora said.

"Stop, sweet mistress, and be satisfied," Gunophilus said.

Pandora said:

"Base vassal, how dare thou presume to speak? Will thou oppose any deed of mine?"

She beat him.

She then said to him:

"How long have you been made a counselor?"

Gunophilus exited, running.

Stesias exposed his chest and said:

"Strike here thy fill, make lavish of my life, so that in my death my love may find relief.

"Lance up my side, so that when my heart leaps out, thou may behold how it is scorched with love, and how in every way it is cross-wounded and scarred with desire.

"There thou shall read my passions deeply engraved, and in the midst thou shall read only Pandora's name."

Pandora said:

"Why do thou tell me about love and fancy's fire?

"The fire of conflict is kindled in my heart, and if thou were not all unarmed, be sure that I would make a trial of thy strength.

"But now the death of some fierce savage beast in blood shall end my fury's tragedy, for fight I must, or else my gall bladder will burst."

In this society, the gall bladder was believed to be the seat of rancor.

Pandora exited.

Stesias said to himself:

"Ah, Pandora, whose ruthless heart is harder than adamant, whose ears are deaf against affection's laments, and whose eyes are blind when sorrow sheds her tears, you are not contented whether I live or I die.

"But fondling — foolishly doting fool — as I am, why do I grieve like this?

"Isn't Pandora the mistress of my life?

"Yes, yes, and every act of hers is just. Her hardest words are only a gentle wind. Her greatest wound is only a pleasing harm.

"Death at her hands is only a second life."

Stesias exited.

Mars descended.

He said, "Mars has forced Pandora contrary to her nature to manage arms and quarrel with her friends.

"And thus I leave her, all incensed with ire.

"Let Sol cool that which I have set on fire."

Mars exited.

CHAPTER 3

— 3.1 —

Alone, Sol sat down in a seat overlooking the scene.

He said:

"In looking down upon this baser world, I long have seen and rued the harms and injuries done to Pandora, but as I myself am inclined by nature, so shall she now become: gentle and kind, abandoning all rancor, pride, and rage.

"And changing from a lion to a lamb, she shall be loving, liberal, and chaste, discreet and patient, merciful and mild, inspired with poetry and prophecy and the virtues appertaining to and appropriate to womanhood."

Pandora and Gunophilus entered the scene.

Already affected by the beneficent influence of Sol, Pandora said:

"Tell me, Gunophilus, how is Stesias doing now? How is he faring with his wound?

"Unhappy me, who so unkindly hurt so kind a friend!

"But Stesias, if thou pardon what is past, I shall reward thy long-enduring suffering with love.

"These eyes that were like two malignant stars shall yield thee comfort with their sweet aspect."

This society believed that the planets and stars influenced human life. Such influence could be benevolent or malignant.

Pandora continued:

"And these my lips, which did blaspheme thy love, shall speak kindly to thee and bless thee with a kiss.

"And this my hand that hurt thy tender side, shall first with herbs cure the wound it made, and then pledge my faith to thee in recompence.

"And thou, Gunophilus, I ask thee to pardon me, who mistreated thee in my witless, unreasoning rage. As time shall yield opportunity, be sure I will not fail to make thee some amends."

Gunophilus replied, "I am so happy in this pleasant calm that former storms of anger are utterly forgot.

The four Utopian shepherds entered the scene. Stesias stood apart from the other shepherds, who knelt.

"We follow you still in hope of grace to come," Learchus said.

"Sweet Pandora! Deign to accept our humble love suits," Iphicles said.

"Grant me love or wound me to the death!" Melos said.

Pandora said:

"Stand up. Pandora is no longer proud but is instead ashamed of the folly of her former deeds."

The three shepherds stood up.

Pandora then said:

"But why does Stesias stand like a man dismayed?"

She said to him:

"Draw near, I say, and thou, with all the rest, forgive the rigor of Pandora's hand, and quite forget the faults of my disdain."

Stesias joined the other shepherds.

Pandora said:

"If all four of you consent, now is the time wherein I'll make amends for my old offence.

"One of you four shall be my mate in wedlock, and all the rest shall be my well-beloved friends.

"But all of you vow here, in the presence of the gods, that when I choose, my choice shall please you all."

Stesias said:

"Then I make my vow by Pallas Athena, O shepherds' Queen, that Stesias will allow and approve Pandora's choice."

Pallas Athena is the goddess of wisdom; Pandora is the Queen of the shepherds.

Stesias continued:

"But if a man succeeds who less deserves to succeed than I do, I'll rather die than hold a grudge or make complaint."

"I swear the same by all our country — our rural — gods," Melos vowed.

"And I swear the same by our Diana's holy head," Iphicles vowed.

Diana is the goddess of the hunt.

"And I swear the same by Ceres and her sacred nymphs," Learchus said.

Ceres is the goddess of agriculture.

Pandora said:

"Then may love and Hymen, god of marriage, bless me in my choice.

"All of you are young and all of you are lovely fair, all of you are kind and courteous and of sweet demeanor, all of you are committed to what is morally right and all of you are valiant, and all of you are in flowering prime.

"But since you grant my will its liberty and allow me to choose as I wish, come, Stesias, and take Pandora by the hand, and with my hand I pledge to you my spotless, unstained faith."

Stesias was now her husband.

"The word has almost slain me with delight," Stesias said.

"The word with sorrow kills me outright," Learchus said.

"O happy Stesias, but unhappy me," Melos said.

Iphicles said, "Come, let us go and weep our lack elsewhere. Stesias has got Pandora from us all."

Learchus, Melos, and Iphicles exited.

Pandora said to Stesias:

"Their sad departure would make my heart grieve, were it not for the joys that I conceive in thee."

She then said:

"Go, go, Gunophilus, without delay, gather for me balm and cooling violets, and our holy herb nicotian [the tobacco plant], and with all of this bring pure honey from the hive, so that I may here compound a wholesome salve to heal the wound inflicted by my unhappy hand."

"I go," Gunophilus said.

He exited.

Stesias said:

"Blest be the hand that made so happy a wound, for in my suffering I have won thy love, and blessed are thou, who having tried my faith, have given admittance to my heart's deserving.

"Now all is well, and all my hurt is whole, and I am in paradise because of my delight.

"Come, lovely spouse, let us go walk in the woods, where warbling birds render in song our happiness, and whistling leaves make music to our mirth, and Flora, goddess of the spring, strews her bower to welcome thee."

Pandora said, "But first, sweet husband, be thou ruled by me: Follow my advice. Go make provisions for some holy rites, so that religious zeal may prosper our new joined love, and by and by I myself will follow thee."

"Don't delay, my dear, for in thy looks I live," Stesias said.

He exited.

Alone, but watched by Sol, Pandora said to herself:

"I feel myself inspired, but I do not know how, nor what it is, unless it is some holy power.

"My heart foretells me many things to come, and I am full of unacquainted, unfamiliar skill, yet such as will not issue from my tongue, but like Sibylla's golden prophecies, affecting rather to be clad in verse — the certain badge of great Apollo's gift — than to be spread and soiled in vulgar words.

"And now to ease the burden of my load, like Sibyl, thus Pandora must begin to prophesy."

The Sybil of Cumae wrote her prophecies on leaves and left them near the opening of the cave that she lived in. If the wind disturbed the leaves, the Sybil did not put them back in the correct order.

The Sybil is sometimes called Sibyl or Sibylla.

Stesias returned and said, "Come, my Pandora. Stesias waits for thee."

Pandora said:

"Peace, man, be silent with reverence here and note my words, for from Pandora speaks the laureate god: Apollo, god of poetry and prophecy."

Pandora prophesized:

"*Utopiae Stesias Poenici solvit amorem,*

"*Numina aelorum dum pia paecipiunt.*

"And backward thus the same, but with double sense.

"*Praecipiunt pia dum caelorum numina, amorem*

"*Solvit phoenici Stesias Utopiae.*"

The prophecy says, "While the pious gods of the Heavens command it, Stesias *solvit amorem* the Phoenix of Utopia."

The phoenix of Utopia is Pandora.

Solvit amorem is a Latin phrase with contradictory meanings: It can mean "he gives love" or "he withdraws love."

Here, Stesias can give his love to Pandora, or he can withdraw it from Pandora. Given that this is a prophecy, he will probably do both.

Stesias solemnly repeated these verses, first forward and then backward, and then he said:

"If *solvere amorem* means 'to give love,' then this prophecy means good to Stesias.

"But if *solvere amorem* means 'to withdraw love,' then it is an ill prophecy to us both.

"But speak, Pandora, while the god of prophecy inspires you."

Pandora prophesied:

"*Idaliis prior hic pueris est: aequoris alti*

"*Pulchrior hec nymphis, et prior Aoniis.*

"And backward thus, but still all one in sense.

"*Aoniis prior, et nymphis hec pulchrior alti*

"*Aequoris est: pueris hic prior Idaliis.*"

Pueris hic prior Idaliis means: This boy is superior to the boys of Idalium.

Idalium is a town sacred to Venus.

Aequoris alti pulchrior hec nymphis, et prior Aoniis means: This girl is more beautiful than the nymphs, and she is superior to the Aonian goddesses.

The Aonian goddesses are the Muses.

Stesias solemnly repeated these verses, first forward and then backward, and then he said:

"Forward and back, these also are alike, and the sense is all one, with only the punctuation changed.

"They only import Pandora's praise and mine."

Pandora said, "Even now my poetic fury begins to retire, and now with Stesias, I will retire from here."

Pandora and Stesias exited.

Venus entered the scene, accompanied by her sons Cupid and Joculus.

Venus said:

"Phoebus, leave. Thou make her too precise: too strait-laced and proper."

The Puritans were known for being precise: strait-laced and proper.

Phoebus is Phoebus Apollo, the Sun-god. Venus was referring to Sol.

Venus continued:

"I'll have her witty, quick and lively, and amorous.

"I'll have her delight in revels and in banqueting, in wanton discourses, in music and merry songs."

Sol descended and said:

"Bright Cyprian Queen, treat Pandora well.

"For although at first Phoebus envied and resented her looks, yet now he admires her glorious hue, and he swears that neither Daphne in the spring, nor glistening Thetis in her orient robe, nor shamefast — that is, blushing — Morning clad in silver clouds, are half as lovely as this earthly saint."

Apollo loved the nymph Daphne and pursued her. She ran from him, and she was transformed into a laurel bush. The laurel became sacred to Apollo.

Thetis is the minor sea-goddess who is the mother of Achilles.

"Thetis" may be an error for "Theia," who was the Greek goddess of sight and the goddess of the blue of the sky. Her "orient robe" may be the sunrise colors after they turn to blue.

Or the goddesses Thetis and Theia may be conflated.

Eos is the goddess of Dawn, and she is the personified Morning. Eos loved Tithonus and made him immortal, but she was unable to give him eternal youth. When he grew old, she gave him the gift of eternal sleep.

Venus said, "And since she is so fair, my beams shall make her light, for Levity is Beauty's waiting-maid."

Sol said, "Make Chastity Pandora's waiting-maid, for modest thoughts suit a woman best."

Venus said:

"Away with chastity and modest thoughts.

"*Quo mihi fortunam si non conceditur uti?*"

The Latin means: Why is fortune mine if it cannot be used?

Venus continued:

"Isn't she young? Then let her go into the world and enjoy it.

"All those who are overly chaste are strumpets and deny such as keep their company."

Being overly chaste and denying lovers what they want can be a sexual fetish involving control over other people.

Venus continued:

"It is not the touching of a woman's hand, not kissing her lips, not hanging about her neck, not a speaking look, no, nor a yielding word, that men expect, anticipate, and need.

"Believe me, Sol, it is more, and if Mars were here, he would protest as much."

Mars and Venus had a famous love affair while Venus was married to Vulcan, the blacksmith god.

Sol said:

"But what is more than this is worse than nought and naught."

Too much of what Venus was advocating would be grossly and sexually immoral.

Sol then said to himself:

"I dare not stay lest she infect me, too."

Sol exited.

Venus said:

"What! Has he gone?

"Then for me, light-footed Joculus, put Pandora in a dancing vein."

Joculus said, "Fair mother, I will make Pandora blithe, and like a satyr she will hop upon these plains."

Satyrs are woodland gods. They sing and dance and chase nymphs.

Joculus exited.

Venus said, "Go, Cupid, and give Pandora all the golden shafts, and she will mistake thee for a forester."

When Cupid shoots a golden arrow at you, you fall in love.

"I will and you shall see her immediately fall in love," Cupid said.

Cupid exited, and Venus ascended.

Venus said to herself, "Here, Venus, sit, and with thy influence govern Pandora, Nature's miracle."

Pandora entered the scene, accompanied by Joculus.

"Please be quiet," Pandora said. "Why should I dance?"

"Thus dance the satyrs on the even lawns," Joculus said.

"Thus, pretty satyr, will Pandora dance," Pandora said.

Cupid entered the scene in time to hear Pandora.

He said, "And thus will Cupid make her melody."

He shot her with a golden arrow.

Pandora, Joculus, and Cupid danced and sang.

Joculus sang:

"*Were I a man I could love thee.*"

In other words: If I were a man, I could love thee.

Joculus was a boy. Or he was a satyr.

Pandora sang:

"*I am a maiden. Will thou have me?*"

Joculus sang:

"*But Stesias saith you are not.*"

A maiden is a young unmarried woman. Pandora and Stesias were wife and husband.

Pandora sang:

"*What then? I care not.*"

Cupid sang:

"*Nor I.*"

Joculus sang:

"*Nor I.*"

Pandora sang:

"*Then merely*

"*Farewell, my maidenhead.*

"*These be all the tears I'll shed;*

"*Turn about and trip it [dance].*"

Venus said, "Cupid and Joculus, come and leave her now."

Cupid and Joculus exited.

Pandora said:

"The boys are gone, and I will follow them. I will not follow them; they are too young.

"What honey thoughts are in Pandora's brain?

"*Hospitis est tepido necte recepta sinu.*"

The Latin means: She was welcomed at night by the warm embrace of her visitor.

Pandora continued:

"Ah, I envy her, why wasn't I so welcomed?

"And so will I be. Where is Iphicles? Where is Melos? Where is Learchus? Where is any of the three?

"Shall I cure the sick? Shall I study poetry? Shall I think of honor and of chastity?

"No. Love is fitter than Pandora's thoughts about honor and of chastity, yet not the love of Stesias alone. Learchus is as fair as Stesias, and Melos is far lovelier than Learchus, but if I might choose, I would have Iphicles. And of them all Stesias deserves the least. Must I be tied to him? No, I'll be loose, as loose as Helen, for I am as fair."

Helen is Helen of Troy, the most beautiful woman in the world and the legitimate wife of Menelaus, King of Sparta. She either willingly or unwillingly went with Paris to Troy and became the cause of the Trojan War.

Of course, this is an anachronism because Pandora is the first, and in this book the only, woman to exist.

Gunophilus returned to the scene and said, "Mistress, here are the herbs for my master's wound."

His master was Stesias, Pandora's husband.

"Pretty Gunophilus, give me the herbs," Pandora said. "Where did thou gather them, my lovely boy?"

"Upon Learchus' plain," Gunophilus said.

"I am afraid that Cupid dances upon the plain," Pandora said. "I see his arrowhead upon the leaves."

"And I see his golden quiver and his bow," Gunophilus said.

Pandora said:

"Thou dissemble, but I mean good sooth: I speak truly.

"These herbs have wrought some wondrous effect. Did they get this virtue from thy lily-white hands?

"Let's see thy hands, my fair Gunophilus."

Gunophilus showed Pandora his hands and said, "It may be the herbs did get their strength from my hands, for I have not washed them for many days."

"Such slender fingers has Jove's Ganymede," Pandora said. "Gunophilus, I am lovesick for thee."

"I wish that I were worthy that you should be sick for me!" Gunophilus said.

"I languish for thee," Pandora said. "Therefore, be my love."

"Better you languish than I be beaten!" Gunophilus said. "Pardon me, I dare not love because of my master."

His master was Stesias, Pandora's husband.

"I'll hide thee in a wood, and keep thee close and secret," Pandora said.

"But what if he goes hunting that way?" Gunophilus asked.

"I'll say thou are a satyr of the woods," Pandora said.

"Then I must have horns," Gunophilus said.

"Aye, so thou shall," Pandora said. "I'll give thee Stesias' horns."

"Why, he has no horns," Gunophilus said.

"But he may have horns shortly," Pandora said.

If Pandora and Gunophilus were to sleep together, Stesias would be a cuckolded husband. People in this society joked that cuckolds had invisible horns growing on their forehead.

"You say the truth, and on that condition I am yours," Gunophilus said.

Learchus entered the scene.

He said to himself:

"I may not speak about love, for I have vowed never to solicit her for love, but instead to rest content.

"Therefore, only gaze, eyes, to please yourselves. Don't let my inward sense know what you see, lest my fancy dote upon her still.

"Pandora is divine, but do not say so, lest that thy heart hear thee and break in twain.

"I may not court her. What a hell is this!"

Pandora said, "Gunophilus, I'll have a banquet immediately. Go, thou, get it ready, and then meet me here."

Gunophilus said:

"I will."

He then said to himself:

"But with your permission, I'll stay a while."

Gunophilus was jealous of Learchus and wanted to keep an eye on him.

"Happy are those who are Pandora's guests," Learchus said.

"Then happy is Learchus," Pandora said. "He is my guest."

Learchus said, "And greater joy do I conceive therein than Tantalus, who feasted with the gods."

Tantalus was so proud that he tried to fool the gods. He killed and cooked his own son, Pelops, and he put the meat into a stew that he served the gods. The gods knew the trick, however, so they did not eat the stew — with the exception of the goddess Demeter, who ate part of Pelops' shoulder. Outraged, the gods brought Pelops to life again and gave him a shoulder made out of ivory, and they sentenced Tantalus to eternal torment in the Land of the Dead. He stands in a stream of water, and branches heavily laden with ripe fruit are overhead, yet Tantalus is eternally thirsty and hungry. Whenever Tantalus bends over to drink from the stream, the water dries up. Whenever Tantalus reaches overhead to seize a piece of fruit, a breeze blows the fruit just out of his reach.

Gunophilus said, "Mistress, the banquet."

"What about the banquet?" Pandora asked.

"You have invited nobody to it," Gunophilus said.

"What's that to you?" Pandora said. "Go and prepare it."

Gunophilus said to himself:

"And in the meantime, you will be in love with him."

He then said out loud:

"Please let me stay, and you order him to prepare the banquet."

"Away, you peasant!" Pandora said.

Gunophilus said sarcastically, "Now she begins to love me."

He exited.

Pandora said, "Learchus, if I had closely noticed this golden hair of yours, I would not have chosen Stesias for my love, but now —"

She sighed.

Learchus said, "Lovely Pandora, if a shepherd's tears may move thee to ruth, pity my state. Make me thy love, although Stesias is thy choice, and I instead of love will honor thee."

"Ruth" is pity.

Pandora said to herself:

"Had he not spoken, I would have courted him."

She then said to Learchus:

"Won't thou say Pandora is too light and promiscuous, if she takes thee instead of Stesias?"

"Rather I'll die than have just such a thought," Learchus said.

"Then, shepherd, this kiss shall be our nuptials," Pandora said.

She kissed him.

"This kiss has made me wealthier than Pan," Learchus said.

Pan is the god of flocks, and thus he is wealthy.

Pandora said:

"Then come again."

She kissed him a second time and said:

"Now be as great as Jove."

Jove is Jupiter.

"Let Stesias never touch these lips again," Learchus said.

Pandora said:

"None but Learchus shall touch these lips of mine.

"Now, sweet love, leave, lest Stesias see thee in this amorous vein.

"But go no farther than thy bower, my love. I'll steal away from Stesias and meet thee soon."

"I will, Pandora, and in preparation for thou coming, I'll strew all my bower with flags and water mints."

Flags and water mints were leaves that were strewn on the floor to prepare for the arrival of an important guest. Water mint leaves and blossoms had a pleasant odor.

He exited.

Pandora said to herself, "A husband? What a foolish word is that! Give me a lover; let the husband go."

Melos and Iphicles entered the scene.

"Iphicles, behold the Heavenly nymph," Melos said.

"We may behold her, but she scorns our love," Iphicles said.

"Are these the shepherds who made love to — that is, flirted with and pursued — me?" Pandora asked.

"Yes, and we are the shepherds who yet love thee still," Melos said.

"I wish that Pandora would regard and consider my love suit to her!" Iphicles said.

Pandora said:

"They look like water nymphs, but they speak like men."

The two shepherds were so much in love that they were in tears.

Pandora said to Melos:

"Thou should be Nature in a man's attire."

Nature is female.

She then said to Iphicles:

"And thou should be young Ganymede, the minion to Jove."

A "minion" is a favorite or a loved one. Ganymede was a catamite: a boy kept for homosexual purposes.

Melos said, "If I were Nature, then I would make a world and give it to thee.

Iphicles said, "If I were Ganymede, then I would leave great Jove in order to follow thee."

Pandora said to herself:

"Melos is loveliest. Melos is my love."

She then said to him:

"Come here, Melos. I must tell thee news, news that is tragic to thee and to thy flock."

She whispered in his ear:

"Melos, I love thee. Meet me in the vale."

A vale is a valley.

She spoke out loud:

"I saw him in the wolf's mouth. Melos, fly."

Melos said, "O that so fair a lamb should be devoured! I'll go and rescue him."

He exited.

Iphicles said to Pandora:

"Could Iphicles go away from thee because of a lamb?

"Let the wolf take all my flock, as long as I have thee!

"Tell me to dive for pearl in the sea ...

"Tell me to fetch the feathers of the Arabian bird ..."

The phoenix was a mythological Arabian bird that lived for five hundred years, burned itself up, and rose reborn from the ashes.

Iphicles continued:

"Tell me to fetch the Golden Apples from the Hesperian wood ..."

The Hesperides were nymphs who guarded a tree that produced golden apples. One of Hercules' labors was to get those golden apples.

Iphicles continued:

"Tell me to fetch the mermaid's mirror ..."

Mermaids and sirens were proud of their beauty and carried a mirror so they could look at themselves.

Iphicles continued:

"Tell me to fetch the goddess Flora's habiliment ..."

Flora's habiliment were spring flowers.

Iphicles continued:

"So I may have Pandora for my love."

Iphicles was willing to do difficult or impossible deeds to win Pandora's love.

Pandora said:

"He who would do all this must love me well, and why should he love me and I not love him?

"Will thou for my sake go into yonder grove? We will sing notes to the wild bird and be as pleasant as the Western wind that kisses flowers and plays wantonly with their leaves."

"Will I?" Iphicles said. "O that Pandora would do that!"

"I will!" Pandora said. "And therefore, follow me, Iphicles."

They exited.

Stesias and Gunophilus entered the scene.

Stesias said:

"Did base Learchus court my Heavenly love?

"Pardon me, Pan, if, to revenge this deed, I shed the blood of that dissembling swain. With jealous fire my heart begins to burn."

Pan is the god of shepherds, and he would not want a shepherd's blood to be shed.

Stesias continued:

"Ah, bring me where he is, Gunophilus, lest he entice Pandora from my bower."

"I don't know where he is, but here he'll be," Gunophilus said. "I must provide the banquet, and I must leave."

Stesias said:

"What! Will the shepherds banquet with my wife? Light Pandora, can thou be thus false?

"Tell me where is this wanton banquet kept so that I may hurl the dishes at their heads, mingle the wine with blood, and end the feast with tragic outcries, like the Theban lord where fair Hippodamia was espoused."

When Pirithous, the King of the Lapiths, married Hippodamia, he invited the half-man, half-horse Centaurs. The Centaur Eurytus attempted to rape Hippodamia, and a battle broke out between the Lapiths and the Centaurs. Pirithous, Theseus (Pirithous' best friend), and other men were able to defeat the Centaurs in a battle that came to be known as the Centauromachy.

The Lapiths lived in Thessaly, and Theseus was the King of Athens, so "Theban lord" may be an error for "Thessalian lord" or "Athenian lord."

Gunophilus said, "The banquet will be held here in this place, for so she ordered me."

"Where might I hide so I can see the banquet?" Stesias asked.

Gunophilus said, "In this cave, for over this they'll sit."

He pointed to the place where Pandora and her guests would sit.

"But then I shall not see them when they kiss," Stesias said.

Gunophilus said, "Yet you may hear what they say; if they kiss, I'll halloo."

"Just do so then, my sweet Gunophilus," Stesias said, "and like a strong wind bursting from the earth, so I will rise out of this hollow vault, making the woods shake with my furious words."

Gunophilus said, "But if they don't come at all, or if when they come they behave chastely and honestly, then don't come out of hiding, lest you, seeming to be jealous, make Pandora overly hate you."

Stesias said, "I won't come out of hiding for all the world unless I hear thee call, or if their wanton speech provokes me to come forth."

Gunophilus said:

"Well, get in hiding, then!"

Stesias hid in the cave, which went down into the earth.

Gunophilus then said:

"Wouldn't it be a pretty jest to bury him alive? I warrant it would be a good while before she would scratch him out of his grave with her fingernails, and yet she might, too, for she has dug such vaults in my face that you may go from my chin to my eyebrows between the skin and the flesh!"

In her fit of anger while Mars controlled her, Pandora had scratched Gunophilus.

Gunophilus then joked to you, the readers, about the "vaults" made by the scratches: They were big enough to store barrels of wine in.

He said:

"Don't wonder at it, good people! I can prove that there have been two or three merchants with me to hire rooms to lay in wine.

"Unfortunately, the storage rooms do not stand as conveniently located as the merchants would wish, for indeed the storage areas are all too near my mouth, and I am a great drinker. If not for that, I would have had a quarter's rent before now.

"Well, be it known to all men that I have done this to cornute — cuckold and put horns on his forehead — my master, for until now I never had the opportunity.

"You would little think that my neck has grown awry with looking back as I have been kissing, for fear that he would come, and yet it is a fair example.

"Beware of kissing, brethren!"

Stesias peeked out of the cave.

Gunophilus said quietly:

"What! Does the cave open? Before Pandora and he shall have finished, Stesias will pick the lock with his horn."

Pandora entered the scene.

She said:

"Now I have played with wanton Iphicles, yes, and kept touch with Melos. Both are pleased. Now, if Learchus were here!

"But wait, I think that here is Gunophilus. I'll go with him."

Quietly, Gunophilus said, "Mistress, my master is in this cave, thinking to meet you and Learchus here."

Quietly, Pandora said:

"What! Is he jealous?

"Come, Gunophilus, in spite of him I'll kiss thee twenty times."

"Look how my lips quiver for fear!" Gunophilus said.

Pandora said loudly, so Stesias could hear, "Where is my husband? Speak, Gunophilus."

"He is in the woods, and he will be here soon," Gunophilus said.

Quietly, Pandora said, "Aye, but he shall not."

Pandora said loudly, so Stesias could hear:

"His fellow swains will meet me in this bower, who for his sake I mean to entertain. If he knew of it, he would meet them here.

"Ah! Wherever he is, may he be safe! Thus I hold up my hands to Heaven for him. Thus I weep for my dear love Stesias!"

"When will the shepherds come?" Gunophilus asked.

Pandora said:

"Immediately. Prepare the banquet right away.

"In the meantime, I'll pray that Stesias may be here."

Quietly, she said:

"Bring Iphicles and Melos with thee, and tell them about my husband. *Descendit ad inferos.*"

The Latin means: He has descended into the infernal regions.

Quietly, Gunophilus asked, "You'll love them then?"

Quietly, Pandora said, "No, only thee, yet let them sit with me."

Quietly, Gunophilus said, "I am content, as long as you just sit with them."

He still loved Pandora, and he was still jealous.

He exited.

Learchus entered the scene.

"Why has Pandora thus deluded me?" Learchus asked.

"Learchus, hush!" Pandora said, speaking in a low voice. "My husband's in this cave, thinking to take us together here!"

"Shall I slay him, and enjoy thee still?" Learchus quietly asked.

Quietly, Pandora said, "No! Let him live, but even if he had Argos' eyes, he would not keep me from Learchus' love. Thus I will hang about Learchus' neck and suck out happiness from forth his lips."

Argos had a hundred eyes. This made him an excellent watchman because while some eyes slept, the other eyes stayed open.

Pandora put her arms around Learchus' neck.

Quietly, Learchus said, "And this shall be the Heaven that I'll aim at."

Gunophilus entered the scene, carrying glasses, etc., for the banquet.

Seeing Pandora and Learchus, Gunophilus said to himself: "*Sic vos non vobis; sic vos non vobis.*"

The Latin means: Thus you [work] not for yourself; thus you [work] not for yourself."

The poet Virgil wrote "*Sic vos non vobis,*" according to Aelius Donatus' *Life of Virgil,* lamenting that he had worked hard creating lines of poetry only for another poet to plagiarize them.

Gunophilus was working hard to set up the banquet and please Pandora, but he was worried that he would not enjoy its benefits. Pandora would kiss other people, including Learchus.

Gunophilus, Pandora, and Learchus were now out of the hearing of Stesias.

"What do thou mean by that?" Learchus asked, overhearing Gunophilus.

"Here is a comment upon my words," Gunophilus said.

He threw a glass down and broke it.

"Why do thou break the glass?" Pandora asked.

Gunophilus said:

"I'll answer your question. Shall I provide a banquet and be cheated of the best dish?"

The best dish was Pandora.

He then said to Learchus:

"I hope, sir, that you have said grace, and now I may fall to."

He took Pandora by the hand and embraced her.

"Away, base swain!" Learchus said.

"Sir, as base as I am, I'll go for current here," Gunophilus said.

He was using metaphors of currency.

"Base" can mean 1) of low birth, or 2) made of base metal (not silver or gold).

"Current" can mean 1) has value, and/or 2) is legal tender.

"What?" Learchus said. "Will Pandora be thus light?"

By "light," he meant wanton and promiscuous.

In his answer, Gunophilus used "light" as referring to weight. Legal currency had to be of the correct weight. Low weight would make a gold coin not legal currency.

Gunophilus said, "O! You stand upon the weight! Well, if she were twenty grains lighter, I would not refuse her, provided always she is not clipped within the ring."

"Grains" means 1) a unit of measurement, and 2) the fork of the body that is made by the legs.

"Lighter" means 1) less in weight, and 2) lustier.

People clipped the edges of gold coins to collect the bits of precious metal, but if they clipped the coin too much and clipped inside the ring or circle near the edge of the coin, the coin would not be legal tender.

The word "ring" can also refer to a vagina. A clipped vagina is not a chaste vagina. Gunophilus wanted a vagina that was loyal to him.

Pandora said:

"Gunophilus, thou are too malapert! Thou are too impudent!"

She whispered to Learchus:

"Think nothing about this, for I cannot get rid of him."

She then said to Gunophilus:

"Sirrah, you had best provide the banquet."

"I will!" Gunophilus said, "And I will do that incontinently — without delay! For indeed I cannot abstain."

He could not abstain from love — or jealousy.

Gunophilus exited.

Pandora said:

"Here, take thou Melos' favor."

Melos had cut off the head of the boar that Pandora had wanted the shepherds to kill. The other shepherds also claimed to have at least a share in the killing of the boar.

She handed Learchus one of her gloves and said:

"Keep it secret, for he and Iphicles will soon be here.

"I don't love them. They both importune me, yet I must act as if I love them both."

Seeing Melos and Iphicles coming toward them from different directions, Pandora said:

"Here they come.

"Welcome, Learchus, to Pandora's feast."

Gunophilus returned, carrying food, etc.

Melos and Iphicles met.

"What is Learchus doing here?" Melos asked.

"Why should Melos banquet with my love?" Iphicles asked.

"My heart rises against this Iphicles," Learchus said.

Every man present was in love with Pandora, and every man was jealous.

Pandora loved every man, and especially whatever man was closest to her.

Pandora said:

"Melos, my love!

"Sit down, sweet Iphicles."

She and Iphicles talked together, apart from the others.

"She daunts — discourages — Learchus with a strange — cold and unfriendly — aspect," Melos said hopefully.

"I don't like that she whispers to him," Learchus said.

Iphicles whispered to Pandora, "I promise you."

"Here's to the health of Stesias, my love," Pandora said. "I wish that he were here to welcome all you three."

"I will go seek him in the busky — bushy — groves," Melos said.

"You will lose your labor then," Gunophilus said. "He is with his flock."

Pandora wept and said, "Aye, he values his flock more than me."

"She weeps," Learchus said.

"Don't weep, Pandora, for he loves thee well," Iphicles said.

"And I love him," Pandora said.

"But why is Melos sad?" Iphicles asked.

"Because of thee I am sad," Melos said. "Thou have injured me."

"Doesn't Melos know that I love him?" Pandora said to him quietly so the other men could not hear her.

"Thou injure me, and I will be revenged!" Iphicles said.

"Has Iphicles forgotten my words?" Pandora asked him quietly so the other men could not hear her.

Gunophilus said to himself, "If I should halloo, they would all be ruined."

If he were to halloo, Pandora's husband, Stesias, would come out of hiding and fight them.

Learchus said to himself, "They both — Melos and Iphicles — are jealous, yet they don't mistrust me!"

Iphicles raised his glass and said, "Here, Melos!"

"I pledge — that is, I toast — thee, Iphicles," Melos said.

Pandora whispered, "Learchus, go. Thou know my mind."

Pretending to be angry, Learchus said out loud:

"Shall I sit here thus to be made a stale: a laughing-stock?"

No one had toasted him.

Learchus then said to himself:

"Lovely Pandora intends to follow me. Farewell, this feast. My banquet has not yet come."

He exited.

"Let him go," Iphicles said.

"Pandora, go with me to Stesias," Melos requested.

"No, rather go with me!" Iphicles said.

"Away, base Iphicles!" Melos said.

"Coward! Keep your hand off me! Or else I'll strike thee down!" Iphicles said.

Pandora said quietly but urgently:

"My husband hears you!"

She then said louder so her husband could hear:

"Will you strive and fight for wine?

"Give us a fresh cup. I will have you two be friends."

Melos said, "I defy thee, Iphicles!"

"I defy thee, Melos!" Iphicles said.

"Both of them are drunk!" Gunophilus said.

Melos asked Pandora, "Is this thy love to me?"

Pandora said:

"Nay, if you fall out with each other and fight, farewell."

She then said to herself:

"Now I will go and meet Learchus."

Pandora exited.

Iphicles said to Melos, "I see thy trickery. Thou shall lack thy will."

He thought that Pandora and Melos had arranged an assignation.

"Follow me if thou dare, and fight it out," Melos said.

"If I dare?" Iphicles said. "Yes, I dare, and I will! Come, thou."

Iphicles and Melos exited.

Gunophilus called, "Halloo! Halloo!"

Stesias came out of the cave.

"Where is the villain who has kissed my love?" Stesias asked.

Gunophilus had told him that he would call "halloo" if someone kissed Pandora.

"Nobody has kissed her, master," Gunophilus said.

"Why did they fight, then?" Stesias asked.

"It was for a cup of wine," Gunophilus said. "They were all drunk."

"Where has my wife gone?" Stesias asked.

"To seek you," Gunophilus answered.

Stesias said:

"Ah! Pandora, pardon me! Thou are chaste."

He then said to Gunophilus:

"Thou made me suspect her, so take thou that."

He beat Gunophilus.

"O master! I did what I did out of good will to you!" Gunophilus said.

"And I beat thee out of good will to her," Stesias said. "What have thou to do between man and wife?"

Gunophilus said to himself, "Too much with the man, and too little with the wife."

They exited.

CHAPTER 4
— 4.1 —

Mercury entered the scene. His Greek name was Hermes, and he was the god of thieves and of eloquence. He was a trickster god.

He said to Venus, "Empress of love, give Hermes permission to reign. My orbit comes next; therefore, resign your position to me."

The planets were ruling Pandora in order: starting with the planet furthest away, Saturn, and ending with the planet closest to the Earth, which was the Moon. The order was Saturn, Jupiter, Mars, Sol (the Sun), Venus, Mercury, and the Moon.

Venus descended.

She said to Mercury, "Ascend, thou winged pursuivant — herald — of Jove."

Venus exited, and Mercury ascended.

Mercury said:

"Now Pandora shall be no more in love, and all these swains who were her favorites shall understand their mistress has played false, and loathing her they will blab all to Stesias, her husband.

"Now Pandora is in my regiment, and I will make her false and full of tricks, thievish, lying, subtle and cunning, and eloquent, for these alone belong — uniquely are relevant — to Mercury."

Melos, Learchus, and Iphicles entered the scene and complained about Pandora.

"Unkind Pandora was unkind to delude me like this," Iphicles said.

"Too kind was Learchus, who has loved her like this," Learchus said.

"Too foolish is Melos, who still dotes on her," Melos said.

"May black be the ivory of her enticing face," Learchus said.

This society valued light-colored skin; it did not value dark-colored skin.

"May the sunshine of her ravishing eyes be dimmed," Melos said.

"May her face be fair, and may her eyes be beautiful!" Learchus said.

"O Iphicles, abjure and reject her," Learchus said. "She is false!"

"To thee, Learchus, and to Melos she is false," Iphicles said.

"Nay, she is false to all of us; she is too false and full of guile," Melos said.

"How many thousand kisses did she give me, and every kiss was mixed with an amorous glance," Learchus said.

"How often have I leaned on her silver breast, with she singing on her lute, and with Melos being the note," Melos said.

The name "Melos" means "song."

"Note" means 1) tune or melody, and/or 2) theme or content.

"But waking, what sweet pastime have I had," Iphicles said, "for love is watchful, and can never sleep."

Melos said, "But before I slept—"

Learchus said, "When I desired—"

"What then?" Iphicles asked.

"*Cetera quis nescit*?" Melos answered.

The Latin means: Who doesn't know the rest?

"Melos anticipated what I would have said," Learchus said.

Iphicles said, "Blush, Iphicles, and in thy rosy cheeks, let all the heat that feeds thy heart appear."

"Don't droop, fair Iphicles, because of Pandora's misdeeds," Learchus said, "but to get revenge for her misdeeds, have recourse to Stesias."

In other words: Tell Stesias about the misdeeds of his wife: Pandora.

"Yes, he shall know she is lascivious," Melos said.

"In this complaint I'll join with thee," Iphicles said. "Let us go."

"Wait, here he comes," Learchus said.

Stesias and Gunophilus entered the scene.

Stesias was congratulating himself on his chaste wife d:

"O Stesias, what a Heavenly love have thou! A love as chaste as is Apollo's tree! As modest as a Vestal Virgin's eye, and yet as bright as glowworms in the night, with which the Morning goddess decks her lover's hair!

"O fair Pandora, blessed Stesias!"

Apollo's tree is the laurel.

Vestal Virgins were maidens who served Vesta, goddess of the hearth.

"O foul Pandora, cursed Stesias!" Iphicles said.

"What do thou mean, Iphicles?" Stesias asked.

Melos said, "Ah! Is she fair who is lascivious? Or is that swain blest whom she makes but a stale: a laughingstock?"

"He means thy love, unhappy Stesias," Learchus said.

Stesias said:

"My love? No, shepherds, this is just a stale, to make me hate Pandora, whom I love."

A "stale" can be 1) a trick, or 2) a laughingstock.

Stesias continued:

"So whispered recently the false Gunophilus."

Stesias believed that Gunophilus had tried to convince him that Pandora was false.

Stesias continued:

"Let it suffice that I don't believe you."

"Love is deaf, blind, and incredulous," Iphicles said. "I never hung about Pandora's neck. She never called me fair and never called thee a black swain."

Melos said, "She did not play music to Melos in her bower, nor is his green bower strewn with primrose leaves."

Melos had strewn primrose leaves in his bower as a way to welcome Pandora.

"I did not kiss her, nor did she call me her love," Learchus said. "Pandora is the love of Stesias."

Learchus, Iphicles, and Melos exited.

Stesias ordered Gunophilus, "Sirrah! Tell your mistress to come here."

"I shall, sir," Gunophilus said.

He exited.

Stesias repeated the words of the other swains:

"'I never hung about Pandora's neck'—

"'She did not play music to Melos in her bower'—

"'I did not kiss her, nor did she call me her love'—"

He then said:

"These words argue that Pandora is light and promiscuous. She played the wanton with these amorous swains.

"By all these streams that interlace these waters, which I hope may be venom to her thirsty soul, I'll be revenged as a shepherd never was!"

Previously, Stesias had said:

"O fair Pandora, blessed Stesias!"

But now he said:

"Now foul Pandora, wicked Stesias!"

Gunophilus returned, escorting Pandora.

Gunophilus said, "Mistress, it is true. I heard the shepherds and what they said to your husband. Don't do anything risky."

Pandora said, "Defenced with her tongue, and guarded with her wit and intelligence, thus goes Pandora to Stesias."

Stesias said to her, "Detested falser! Detested deceiver who to Stesias' eyes are more infectious than the basilisk."

The basilisk was a mythological monster that could kill with a glance.

Pandora said:

"Gunophilus, Pandora is undone! She is destroyed! Her love, her joy, her life has lost his wits!"

She was referring to Stesias.

Pandora continued:

"Offer a kid goat in Aesculapius' temple, so that he may cure him, lest I die outright."

Gunophilus said to himself, "I'll offer it to Aesculapius, but he shall not have it, for when Stesias comes to himself, I must answer for the kid goat."

Stesias would not want to lose a kid goat.

"Go, I say!" Pandora ordered Gunophilus.

Stesias ordered Gunophilus:

"Stay!"

He then said to Pandora:

"I am well. It is thou who make me rave.

"Thou played the wanton woman with my fellow swains."

Pandora said to herself:

"Then die, Pandora!"

She said to her husband:

"Are thou in thy wits, and thou call me a wanton woman?"

She fell down.

Gunophilus said, "O master! What have you done?"

"Divine Pandora!" Stesias said. "Rise and pardon me!"

Pandora said, "I cannot but forgive thee, Stesias, but by this light, if —"

Gunophilus said, "Look how she closes her eyes."

He was encouraging Stesias to believe that Pandora, now under the influence of the trickster god Mercury, had really fainted.

"Wait, my love!" Stesias said. "I know it was their — the other shepherds' — trick to make me jealous."

Pandora said:

"He who will win me must have Stesias' shape, such golden hair, such alabaster looks.

"Do thou want to know why I did not love Jupiter? Because he was unlike my Stesias."

Stesias said, "Was ever a simple shepherd as abused as I? All three affirmed that Pandora held them dear."

Pandora said:

"It was to bring me into disgrace with thee, so that they might have some hope I would be theirs.

"I cannot walk anywhere but they importune me to love them. How many amorous letters have they sent! What gifts! Yet all in vain.

"To prove that this is true, I'll bear this slander with a patient mind, I'll speak to them all with fair words, and before the sun goes down, I'll bring thee to where they are accustomed to lie in wait for me, to rob me of my honor in the groves."

Stesias said:

"Do so, sweet wife, and they shall pay for it dearly.

"I cannot stay here, for my sheep must go to the sheepfold."

He exited.

Pandora said:

"Go, Stesias, as simple as a sheep.

"And now, Pandora, summon all thy wits so you can be revenged on these long-tongued, too-talkative swains.

"Gunophilus, bear this ring to Iphicles. Tell him I rave and languish for his love. Tell him to meet me in this meadow alone, and swear that his fellows have deluded him."

She handed Gunophilus a ring and continued:

"Bear this to Melos."

She handed Gunophilus a bloody handkerchief and continued:

"Say that for his sake I stabbed myself, and had thou not been near, I would have been dead, but yet I am alive, calling for Melos, the only man whom I love.

"And to Learchus bear these passionate lines, which, if he is not made of flint, will make him come."

She handed Gunophilus a letter.

Gunophilus said, "I will, and you shall see how cunningly I'll treat them. Stay here, and I will send them to you one after another, and then you shall treat them as your wisdom shall think good."

He exited.

Pandora said to herself:

"That letter I penned, fearing the worst, and I dipped the handkerchief in the lambkin's blood.

"For Iphicles, even if he were entirely made of iron, my ring is adamant — a magnet — to draw him forth.

"Let women learn from me how to be revenged.

"I'll make these shepherds bite their tongues and eat their words, yes, and swear to my husband that all is false.

"My wit is pliant and my invention is sharp, and they will make these shepherds who injure me mere novices in deception."

Seeing Iphicles approaching, she said:

"Young Iphicles must have boasted that I favored him!

"Here I protest as Helen did to her love:

"*Oscula luctanti tantummodo pauca protervus abstulit: ulterius, nil habet ille mei.*"

The Latin means: He took only a few kisses from me, who struggled; other than those kisses, he got nothing.

Pandora then said:

"And what's a kiss? Too much for Iphicles!"

Iphicles entered the scene and said:

"Melos is wily, and Learchus is false. Here is Pandora's ring, and she is mine! It was a stratagem laid for my love.

"Foolish Iphicles, what have thou done? Must thou betray her to Stesias?"

Pandora pretended not to see Iphicles and said, so he could overhear her:

"Here I will sit until I see Iphicles, sighing my breath, and weeping out my heart-blood.

"Go, soul, and fly to my dearest love, who is a fairer subject than Elysium."

Elysium is the good and pleasant section of the Underworld. Other parts of the Underworld punish sinners.

Iphicles asked himself:

"Can I hear this? Can I view her?"

Pandora looked at him, and he said:

"O no!"

Pandora said, "But I will look at thee, my sweet Iphicles! Thy looks are medicine to me; allow me to gaze at thee. It is for thy sake that I am thus distempered and made ill."

"Pale are my looks when they witness my wrongdoing," Iphicles said.

"And my looks are pale to show my love," Pandora said. "Lovers are pale."

Iphicles said, "And so is Iphicles."

"And so is Pandora," she said. "Let me kiss my love, and add a better color to his cheeks."

"Bury all thy anger in this kiss, and don't checkmate and confound me by uttering my offence," Iphicles said.

Pandora said:

"Who can be angry with one whom she loves?

"I would rather have no thoughts at all than have just one ill thought about my Iphicles.

"Go to Stesias and deny thy words thou spoke to him, for he has thrust me from his cabinet: his habitation. And as I have loved thee in the past, I will love thee still.

"Don't delay. Make haste, gentle Iphicles, and meet me on the sedgy banks of the Enipeus River.

Sedges are grassy plants that grow on wet ground.

"When shall I meet thee?" Iphicles said. "Tell me, my bright love."

"At midnight, Iphicles," Pandora said. "Until then, farewell!"

"Farewell, Pandora!" Iphicles said. "I'll go to Stesias."

He exited.

Pandora said to herself:

"Thus I will serve them all.

"Now, Melos, come to me. I love thee, too — as much as I love Iphicles."

Carrying the bloody handkerchief and some medicinal herbs, Melos said to himself:

"This is Pandora's blood; make haste, Melos, make haste! And in her presence lance thy flesh as deep.

"Wicked Learchus, subtle Iphicles, you have undone and ruined me with your far-reaching wit."

Pandora said:

"Gunophilus! Where is Gunophilus? Give me the knife thou pulled from my breast. Melos has gone, and left Pandora here.

"Witness, you wounds, and witness, you silver streams of tears, that I am true, to Melos only true, and he has betrayed me to Stesias."

"Forgive me, love," Melos said. "It was not I alone. It was also Learchus and false Iphicles."

Pandora said:

"It is not Learchus, nor that Iphicles, who grieves me, but it grieves me that Melos is unkind —

"Melos, for whom Pandora strained her voice, playing with every letter of his name ...

"Melos, for whom Pandora made this wound ...

"Melos, for whom Pandora now will die!"

She pretended to be about to commit suicide.

Melos said:

"Divine Pandora, stop thy desperate hand!

"May summer's lightning burn our autumn crop, may the thunder's teeth plow up our fairest groves, may the scorching sunbeams dry up all our springs, and may rough winds blast the beauty of our plains, if Melos does not love thee more than he loves his heart."

"So Melos swears, but it is a lovers' oath," Pandora said.

"Once guilty, and suspected evermore!" Melos said. "I'll never be guilty anymore, so do not suspect me."

Pandora said:

"I do not suspect thee anymore, so don't mistrust me."

"Learchus never touched Pandora's lips.

"Nor did Iphicles receive a friendly word from me.

"Melos has all my favors, and for all, do only this one thing, and I'll be only thine: Go to Stesias and deny thy words, and as the sun goes down, I'll meet thee here."

"I will, Pandora," Melos said, "and to cure thy wound, receive these virtuous herbs that I have found."

Melos exited.

Pandora said:

"Melos is a pretty swain worthy of Pandora's love!

"But I have written to Learchus, I, and I will keep my promise although I die, which is to treat him as he treated me — badly."

Learchus and Gunophilus entered the scene.

Learchus read out loud Pandora's letter, which he was carrying:

"'*Learchus, my love! Learchus!*'"

He said:

"The iteration of my name argues her affection!"

He read out loud:

"'*Was it my desert? Did I deserve it? Thine, alas! Pandora.*'"

He said:

"It was my destiny to be credulous to these miscreants. I believed those villains."

Learchus again believed that Pandora loved him. He did not now believe the other shepherds, who had believed that Pandora had tricked them, including Learchus, into believing that she loved them, when she did not.

Pandora pretended to write.

Gunophilus said, "Look, look, she is writing to you again."

"What! Has Learchus come?" Pandora said. "Then my tongue shall declaim. Yet I am bashful and afraid to speak."

"Don't blush, Pandora," Learchus said. "Who has made the most fault?"

"I who solicit thee, who does not love me," Pandora said.

"I who betrayed thee, who did not offend," Learchus said.

"Learchus, pardon me!" Pandora said.

"Pandora, pardon me!" Learchus said.

Gunophilus said to himself, "All friends! And so they kissed."

Pandora said:

"I can only smile to think thou were deceived.

"Learchus, thou must go to my husband immediately and say that thou are sorry for thy words, and in the evening, I'll meet thee again, under the same grove where we both sat last."

Learchus said:

"I will, Pandora."

Pandora had arranged to meet Learchus at a grove in the evening. She had arranged to meet Melos here when the Sun went down. She had arranged to meet Iphicles on the sedgy banks of the Enipeus River at midnight.

Learchus then said:

"But look where your husband comes."

Pandora said:

"Then give me permission to lie and dissemble."

Stesias entered the scene, but he was a short distance away.

Pandora said loudly so that her husband would hear, "It is not thy sorrow that can make amends. If I were a man, thou would repent thy words!"

Stesias walked over to them and said, "Learchus, will you stand to your words? Do you still say that your words were true?"

"O Stesias!" Learchus said. "Pardon me. It was their — the other shepherds' — deceit. I am sorry that I injured her."

Stesias said, "They lay the fault on thee, and thou on them. But take thee that."

He struck Learchus.

Pandora said:

"Ah, Stesias, stop. You shall not fight for me.

"Go, go, Learchus. I am Stesias.'"

"Are thou?" Learchus asked.

Gunophilus said quietly to him, "No, no, Learchus, she does just say so."

Stesias said:

"Get off of my ground, Learchus. Stay away from my land, and from henceforward do not come near my lawns."

"Lawns" are untilled land.

Stesias continued:

"Pandora, come!

"Gunophilus, let's go!"

"Learchus, meet me soon," Pandora said quietly to Learchus. "The time draws nigh."

Stesias exited, then Gunophilus exited, and then Pandora exited.

Learchus said: "The time draws nigh! I wish that the time were now! I go to meet Pandora at the grove."

He exited.

Melos arrived at the place where Pandora had said she would meet him.

He said:

"When will the sun go down? Fly, Phoebus, fly!"

Phoebus Apollo, the Sun-god, drove the Sun-chariot across the sky each day. Melos wanted the time to pass quickly so that he could meet Pandora.

Melos continued:

"I wish that thy steeds were winged with my swift thoughts.

"Now thou should fall in Thetis' azure — bright blue — arms, and now I would fall in Pandora's lap."

The minor sea-goddess Thetis married a mortal man named Peleus, and Apollo sang at their wedding.

"Thetis" may be an error for "Theia," a Greek goddess who may be regarded as being blue. Her husband was Hyperion, and she was the goddess of sight and the goddess of the blue of the sky. Apollo's falling into her arms may be a metaphor for the sun setting.

Or the goddesses Thetis and Theia may be conflated.

Iphicles entered the scene and said, "Why did Jupiter create the day? Sweet is the night when every creature sleeps. Come, night. Come, gentle night, for thee I wait."

"Why does Iphicles desire the night?" Melos asked.

Startled by Melos' voice, Iphicles said:

"Who's that? Melos? Thy words did make me afraid.

"I wish for midnight just to take the wolf, which kills my sheep and for which I make a snare.

"Melos, farewell, I must go to watch my flocks."

Iphicles exited.

Melos said:

"And I to meet my love! Here she will meet me straightaway.

"See where she comes, hiding her blushing eyes."

Stesias entered the scene, wearing women's apparel, including a veil.

Melos said, "My love Pandora, for whose sake I live! Don't hide thy beauty, which is Melos' Sun. Here is no one but us two, so lay aside thy veil."

Stesias said, "Here is Stesias! Melos, you are deceived!"

He struck Melos.

"Pandora has deceived me," Melos said. "I am undone and ruined!"

He exited.

Stesias said, "I will not deceive you, sir. My meaning is straightforward."

His meaning was that he wanted to beat Stesias.

Stesias exited, chasing after Melos.

Pandora and Gunophilus entered the scene.

Pandora said, "Come, have thou all Stesias' jewels and his pearls?"

Mercury was the god of thieves as well as the god of trickery.

Gunophilus said, "Aye, all! But tell me which way we shall go."

Pandora said, "To the seaside, and we will take shipping straightaway."

They would sail away with the stolen jewels.

Gunophilus said, "Well, I am revenged at last on my master. I pray to God that I may be thus even with all my enemies, only to run away with their wives."

"Gunophilus, for thee I have done this," Pandora said.

Gunophilus said, "Aye, and for yourself, too. I am sure you will not beg by the way."

"For thee, I'll beg and die, Gunophilus!" Pandora said.

Gunophilus said, "Aye, so I think; the world is so hard that if you beg, you may be sure to be starved."

"I ask thee to be not so churlish," Pandora said.

Gunophilus said:

"This is but mirth; don't you know *comes facetus est tanquam vehiculus in via*?"

He translated:

"A merry companion is as good as a wagon on the road."

He then explained:

"For you shall be sure to ride although you go on foot."

The Latin *rideo* means "I laugh."

Yes, a merry companion can make a hard journey much easier.

"Gunophilus, setting this mirth aside, don't thou love me more than all the world?" Pandora asked.

Gunophilus said, "Be you as steadfast to me as I'll be to you, and we two will go to the world's end; and yet we cannot, for the world is round, and seeing it is round, let's dance in the circle. Come, turn about."

They danced.

"When I forsake thee, then Heaven itself shall fall," Pandora said.

Gunophilus said, "No, God forbid, then perhaps we should have larks."

If Heaven falls, the birds will fall with it.

A proverb stated, "If the sky falls, we shall have larks."

The proverb meant that something — in this case, Pandora's forsaking Gunophilus — was very unlikely to occur.

They exited.

Stesias entered the scene. He was still wearing women's apparel.

"This is Enipeus' bank," he said. "Here she should be."

Pandora, who was using her husband to get vengeance on the shepherds who had told on her, had told her husband that she had arranged to meet Iphicles here.

Iphicles entered the scene.

He said:

"What! Is it midnight? Time has been my friend. Come, sweet Pandora, all is safe and quiet."

Stesias moved away.

Iphicles asked:

"Whither flies my love?"

"Follow me, follow me," Stesias said. "Here comes Stesias!"

"She has betrayed me," Iphicles said. "Where shall I fly?"

Stesias struck Iphicles, and then he said, "Either to the river, or else to thy grave."

Iphicles exited, running.

Learchus entered the scene.

He said, "The evening has passed, yes, and midnight is at hand. And yet Pandora has not come to the grove."

"But Stesias is her deputy," Stesias said. "He comes, and with his shepherd's hook, he greets Learchus thus."

A shepherd's hook is a staff with a curved end, which was useful for managing sheep.

He struck Learchus.

"Pardon me, Stesias," Learchus said. "It was Pandora's wiles that have betrayed me. Don't trust her, for she is false."

Stesias said:

"Why do thou tell me the contrary to the truth?

"Take that."

He struck Learchus again.

Stesias continued:

"She is honest, but thou would seduce her. Stay away from my grove, stay off of my land. Didn't I give thee warning?"

Stesias drove Learchus away. They exited with Stesias running after and hitting Learchus.

CHAPTER 5

— 5.1 —

Luna is the Moon, and another of her names is Cynthia. The word "lunatic" comes from her name.

She arrived, and Mercury descended, bowed to Luna, and exited.

Luna said to herself:

"Now that the other planets' influence is done, to Cynthia, the lowest of the wandering stars and thus the closest planet to Earth, has beauteous Pandora been given in charge.

"And as I am, so shall Pandora be, newfangled and addicted to novelty, fickle, slothful, foolish, and mad, in spite of Nature, who envies us all."

Nature is unlikely to envy the seven planets.

Pandora and Gunophilus entered the scene. They had stolen Stesias' jewels and were running away from him. They wanted to reach the seashore and leave in a ship.

Gunophilus said, "Come, come, Pandora, we must make more haste, or Stesias will overtake us both."

"I cannot go any faster," Pandora said. "I must rest."

She lay down.

"We are almost at the seaside," Gunophilus said. "I ask thee to please rise."

"I am faint and weary," Pandora said. "Let me sleep."

"Pandora, if thou love me, let us go," Gunophilus said.

"Why do thou awaken me?" Pandora said. "I'll remember this."

"What! Are you angry with me?" Gunophilus asked.

Pandora said:

"No, I am angry with myself for loving such a swain.

"What fury made me dote upon these looks? Like winter's picture are his withered cheeks. His hair is like a raven's plumes."

Gunophilus touched her shoulder.

Pandora said:

"Ah! Don't touch me!

"His hands are like the fins of some foul fish.

"Look how he moves, like an aged ape! Over the chain, Jack! Or I'll make thee leap!"

"Over the chain" was a trick that monkeys — a jackanapes is a tame monkey — performed.

Luna was influencing Pandora and making her see Gunophilus as an old man rather than the youth he was.

"What a sudden change is here!" Gunophilus said.

Pandora said:

"Now he swears by his ten bones — his ten fingers.

"Down, I say!"

Gunophilus said, "Didn't I tell you I should have larks?"

He had said that he would have larks when Pandora betrayed him and Heaven fell.

Pandora said:

"Where are the larks? Come, we'll go catch some straightaway!

"No, let us go fishing with a net! With a net? No, an angle — a fishing rod — is enough. An angle, a net, no, none of both. I'll wade into the water, water is fair, and I'll stroke the fishes underneath the gills.

"But first I'll go hunting in the wood. I don't like hunting; let me have a hawk.

"What will thou say if I love thee still?"

"I will say anything, whatever you want!" Gunophilus said.

Pandora said:

"But shall I have a gown of oaken leaves, a chaplet of red berries, and a fan made of the morning dew to cool my face?

"How often will you kiss me in an hour?

"And where shall we sit until the sun is down? For *Nocte latent mendae.*"

The Latin means: Blemishes are hidden by night.

Gunophilus asked, "What then?"

Pandora said:

"I will not kiss thee until the sun is down; whoever are deformed, the night will cover thee.

"We women must be modest in the day. Don't tempt me until the evening comes."

Gunophilus said:

"*Lucretia tota sis licet usque die: Thaida nocte volo.*

"Hate me during the days, and love me in the night."

The Latin means: During the day, be Lucretia. At night, I want Thais.

Lucretia was a virtuous Roman lady, and Thais was an unvirtuous Roman courtesan — a nice word for "prostitute."

Pandora said:

"Do thou call me Thais? Go, and do not love me.

"I am not Thais, I'll be Lucretia, I will.

"Give me a knife, and for my chastity I'll die to be canonized a saint."

After being raped by Sextus Tarquinius, the son of King Lucius Tarquinius Superbus, Lucretia told her story to others and then committed suicide with a knife. The Romans then threw out King Lucius Tarquinius Superbus and started the Roman Republic.

Gunophilus asked, "But will you love me when the sun is down?"

"No, but I will not!" Pandora said.

"Didn't you promise me?" Gunophilus asked.

"No! Aye! I didn't see thee until now," Pandora said.

The influence of the Moon was working on her.

"Do you see me now?" Gunophilus asked.

"Aye, and I loath thee!" Pandora said.

"Likely I was a spirit all this while?" Gunophilus asked.

"A spirit! A spirit!" Pandora said. "Where may I flee?"

Stesias entered the scene. He was wearing his own attire.

"I see Pandora and Gunophilus," Stesias said.

"And I see Stesias," Pandora said. "Welcome, Stesias!"

Stesias said:

"Gunophilus, thou have inveigled her and lured her away, and thou have robbed me of my treasure and my wife."

Another person who did this was Paris, Prince of Troy, who ran away with the wife and some of the treasure of Menelaus, King of Sparta, thus causing the Trojan War.

Stesias continued:

"I'll strip thee to the skin for this offence, and put thee in a wood to be devoured by empty tigers and by hungry wolves, nor shall thy sad looks move me to ruth and pity."

Gunophilus said:

"Pardon me, master. Pandora is lunatic, foolish, and frantic, and I followed her only so I could save the goods — your jewels — and bring her back.

"Why, do you think I would run away with her?"

Pandora said:

"He need not, for I'll run away with him.

"And yet I will go home with Stesias, so I shall have a white lamb colored black, two little sparrows, and a spotted fawn."

"I fear that what Gunophilus reports is too true," Stesias said. "Pandora is lunatic."

Gunophilus said, "Nay, stay a while, and you shall see her dance."

Pandora said:

"No, no, I will not dance, but I will sing."

She sang:

"*Stesias has a white hand,*

"*But his nails [fingernails] are black;*

"*His fingers are long and small,*

"*Shall I make them crack?*"

A lover's game was to pull the loved one's fingers and make them crack.

"*One, two, and three;*

"*I love him, and he loves me.*

"*Beware of the shepherd's hook;*

"*I'll tell you one thing,*

"*If you ask me why I sing,*

"*I say you may go look.*"

The last line meant: I won't tell you.

"Pandora, speak," Stesias said. "Do thou love Gunophilus?"

Pandora said:

"Aye, if he is a fish, for fish is fine.

"Sweet Stesias, help me to a whiting-mop."

A whiting-mop was an immature white-fleshed fish; it was also a term of endearment for a young girl.

"Help me to a whiting-mop" may mean "Get me pregnant with a girl baby."

"Now I perceive that she is lunatic," Stesias said. "What may I do to bring her to her wits?"

Gunophilus said, "Speak, gentle master, and entreat her with fair words."

"Pandora! My love, Pandora!" Stesias said.

"I'll not be fair," Pandora said. "Why do you call me your love? Love is a little boy, and I am not!"

Love is another name for Cupid, son of Venus.

Stesias said, "I will allure her with fair promises, and when I have her in my leafy bower, I will pray to our water nymphs and sylvan — woodland — gods to cure her of this piteous lunacy."

Pandora said, "Give me a running stream in both my hands, a blue kingfisher, and a pebble stone, and I'll catch butterflies upon the sand, and thou, Gunophilus, shall clip their wings."

Stesias said, "I'll give thee streams whose pebbles shall be pearl, lovebirds whose feathers shall be beaten gold, musk-flies with amber berries in their mouths, milk-white squirrels, singing popinjays, a boat of dear skins, and a fleeting — that is, wandering — isle, a sugar cane, and a line of twisted silk."

In mythology, Delos was an island that floated on the surface of the sea until the sea-god Poseidon, whose Roman name is Neptune, fastened it to the bottom of the sea. The twins Apollo and Artemis (Roman name: Diana) were born there.

"Where are all these?" Pandora asked.

"I have them in my bower," Stesias said. "Come, follow me."

Pandora said:

"Streams with pearls? Birds with golden feathers? Musk-flies, and amber berries? White squirrels, and singing popinjays? A boat of dear skins?

"Come, I'll go! I'll go!"

Stesias and Pandora exited.

Gunophilus said to himself:

"I was never in love with her until now. O absolute, perfect Pandora because foolish Pandora, for folly is women's perfection. To talk idly, to look wildly, to laugh at every breath and play with a feather — these are things that would make a Stoic fall in love, yes, and thou thyself fall in love:

"*O Marce fili, annum iam audientem Cratippum, idque Athenis.*"

The Latin, translated by Walter Miller, means: "My dear son Marcus, you have now been studying a full year under Cratippus, and that too in Athens."

Cratippus of Pergamon was a Peripatetic philosopher whom Cicero greatly respected.

Gunophilus has been learning about women recently.

He continued:

"Gravity in a woman is like a gray beard upon a breaching boy's chin, which a good schoolmaster would cause to be clipped, and the wise husband would cause to be avoided."

To "avoid" is to "refute." A wise husband would be able to show that he is more intelligent than his wife.

This society regards a good wife as an obedient wife. This society also regards a good husband as one who is more intelligent than his wife.

A breeching boy is a boy who is still young enough to be whipped.

Melos, Iphicles, and Learchus entered the scene.

Melos was carrying the bloody handkerchief, Iphicles was carrying Pandora's ring, and Learchus was carrying Pandora's letter to him.

Melos asked, "Gunophilus, where is thy mistress, Pandora?"

"She is catching a blue kingfisher," Gunophilus said.

"Tell us where she is," Iphicles requested.

"She is gathering little pebbles," Gunophilus said.

"What!" Learchus said. "Do thou mock us?"

"No," Gunophilus said, "but if she were here, she would make mows — that is, make faces — at the proudest of you."

"What do thou mean by this?" Melos asked.

"I mean that my mistress has become foolish," Gunophilus said.

"A just reward for one as false as she," Iphicles said.

"May such fortune fall to those who intend us ill," Melos said.

"Never were simple shepherds so abused," Learchus said.

"Gunophilus, thou have betrayed us all," Iphicles said. "Thou brought this ring from her to me, which made me come."

"And thou brought this bloody handkerchief to me," Melos said.

"And thou brought this flattering letter to me," Learchus said.

Gunophilus said to Iphicles:

"Why, I brought you the ring, thinking that you and she should be married together."

He said to Melos:

"And being hurt, as she told me, I had thought she had sent for you as a surgeon."

"But why did thou bring me this letter?" Learchus asked.

Gunophilus said to Learchus:

"Only to notify you that she was in health, as I was at the bringing hereof."

He then said to all three shepherds:

"And thus being loath to trouble you, I commit you to God. Yours, as his own, Gunophilus."

This was a parody of how many letters in this society ended.

Gunophilus exited.

"The wicked youngling flouts and mocks us," Melos said. "Let him go!"

Learchus prayed to the god of shepherds and flocks, "Immortal Pan, wherever this lad remains, revenge the wrong that he has done thy swains."

Melos said, "O that a creature so divine as Pandora, whose beauty might force the Heavens to blush, and whose beauty might make fair Nature angry to the heart that she — Nature — has made Pandora only for Pandora to obscure Nature herself, should be so fickle and so full of slights, and feigning love to all, love none at all."

Nature is unlikely to be jealous of her creation: Pandora.

Iphicles said, "Had Pandora been constant and loyal to Iphicles, I would have clad her in sweet Flora's robes. I would have set Diana's garland on her head, I would have made her sole mistress of my wanton flock, and I would sing in honor of her deity, whereas now with tears I curse Pandora's name."

Learchus said:

"The springs smiled to see Pandora's face and leapt above the banks to touch her lips, the proud plains danced with Pandora's weight, the joyous trees bowed when she came near, and in the murmur of their whispering leaves, seemed to say, 'Pandora is our Queen!'

"All of these witnessed how fair and beautiful she was, but now they only witness how false and treacherous she is!"

Learchus was speaking for the springs, the plains, and the trees, but Nature is a better spokesperson for them.

Melos said, "Here I abjure Pandora, and I protest that I will live forever in a single life."

"Learchus makes the same vow to great Pan," Learchus said.

"And so does Iphicles, although sorely against his will," Iphicles said.

Learchus said:

"In witness of my vow, I rend these lines."

He tore up Pandora's letter to him and threw the pieces into the air, saying:

"O thus be my love dispersed into the air!"

Melos threw Pandora's bloody handkerchief on the ground and said, "May here lie the bloody handkerchief that she sent to me, and with it my affection, and my love."

Iphicles broke Pandora's ring and said, "Break, break, Pandora's ring; and with it break Pandora's love, that almost burst my heart."

Stesias, Pandora, and Gunophilus entered the scene.

"Ah, to where runs my love?" Stesias said. "Pandora! Stay! Gentle Pandora, stay! Don't run so fast."

Pandora said:

"Shall I not stamp upon the ground? I will! Who says Pandora shall not rend her hair? Where is the grove that asked me how I did?"

Some gods have spoken out of a bush or a grove. In Exodus 3, God speaks to Moses from a burning bush. The rustling of the leaves in the Grove of Dodona was interpreted by the oracle.

Pandora continued:

"Give me an angle — a fishing pole — for the fish will bite."

"Look how Pandora raves!" Melos said. "Now she is stark mad."

"Because of you, she raves, you who meant to ravish her," Stesias said. "Help to recover her or else you die!"

"May she with raving die!" Learchus said. "So do what thou dare to do."

"She overreached and outwitted us with deceitful guile," Iphicles said, "and Pan, to whom we prayed, has wrought revenge."

Pandora said:

"I'll have the ocean put into a glass, and I'll drink it to the health of Stesias.

"Thy head is full of hedeockes, Iphicles. So, shake them off."

"Hedeockes" may be "head 'ocks," or head-locks, which may be 1) locks of hair, and/or 2) metaphorical locks that bind the mind.

Or, given Pandora's preoccupation with fishing, it may mean "haddocks."

Pandora then said to Iphicles:

"Now let me see thy hand."

She examined his hand and said:

"Look where a biasing star is in this line, and in the other line two and twenty sons."

"Sons" may be "suns."

"Come, come, Pandora. Sleep within my arms," Stesias said.

Pandora said:

"Thine arms are firebrands! Where's Gunophilus?

"Go kiss the echo, and bid Love untruss."

Echo was a nymph who loved Narcissus, who loved himself. Echo wasted away because of her unrequited love until only her voice — an echo — remained. Echoes cannot be kissed.

Love is Cupid, a son of Venus. To "untruss" is to "undress."

Pandora continued:

"Go fetch the Black Goat with the brazen heel, and tell the bellwether I do not hear him."

Goats were associated with lustiness, and bellwethers are sheep that lead a flock and on whose neck a bell is hung.

In Greek mythology, an Empusa was a female vampiric being that had a bronze (or copper) leg and could change its shape into various animals. She seduced young men and then drank their blood and feasted on their flesh.

"Wether" means a castrated ram. The bellwether wore a bell.

Pandora continued: "Not, not, not, that you should not come to me this night, not at all, at all, at all."

She slept.

Gunophilus said, "She is asleep, master. Shall I wake her?"

"O no, Gunophilus," Stesias said. "There let her sleep, and let us pray that she may be cured."

"Stesias, thou pity her who does not love thee," Learchus said.

"The words we told thee, Stesias, were too true," Melos said.

Iphicles said:

"Never did Iphicles dissemble yet.'

Ahem. He had attempted to seduce Pandora without her husband knowing. So had Learchus, Melos, and Gunophilus. All of these men had dissembled to Stesias.

Iphicles continued:

"Believe me, Stesias, she has been untrue."

"Will you yet slay me with your slanderous words?" Stesias said. "Didn't you all swear that Pandora was chaste?"

Learchus said:

"It was her subtle, cunning wit that made us swear.

"For, Stesias, know that she showed love to us all, and she separately sent for us by this swain: Gunophilus.

"And to me he brought such honey lines in a letter from her that overcome by them, I flew to her bower.

"Pandora, when I came, swore that she loved me alone, willing me to deny the words I spoke to you, and she said that at night she would meet me in the grove.

"All this means simply: Lo! I was betrayed."

Melos said, "Gunophilus brought me a bloody cloth, saying that for my love Pandora was almost slain. And when I came to her, she treated me as she treated this swain Learchus, protesting love for me, and appointing me to come to this place."

Iphicles said:

"And by this bearer — Gunophilus — I received a ring, and many a loving word that drew me forth.

"O that a woman should dissemble so!

"She then forswore Learchus and this swain — Melos — saying that Iphicles was only hers, whereat I promised to deny my words, and she promised to meet me at the banks of the Enipeus River."

Stesias asked Gunophilus, "Were thou the messenger to them all?"

Gunophilus said:

"I was, and all that they have said is true. She did not love you, nor them, but me alone.

"How often has she run up and down the lawns, calling aloud, 'Where is Gunophilus?'"

Stesias said to himself, "Ah! How my heart swells at these miscreants' words!"

"Come, let us leave him in this pensive mood," Melos said.

"Fret, Stesias, fret, while we dance on the plain," Learchus said.

"Such fortune happens to incredulous swains," Melos said.

"Sweet is a single life," Iphicles said. "Stesias, farewell."

Melos, Learchus, and Iphicles exited.

Stesias said:

"Go, life; fly, soul; go, wretched Stesias!

"Curst be Utopia for Pandora's sake!

"Let wild boars with their tusks plow up my lawns.

"Let devouring wolves come shake my tender lambs, drive my goats up to some steep rock, and let them fall down headlong in the sea.

"She shall not live, nor shall thou, Gunophilus, to triumph in poor Stesias' overthrow."

Stesias moved toward Pandora, intending to kill her.

The seven planets entered the scene, with Luna descending from above.

"Stop, shepherd!" Saturn said. "Stop!"

"Do not hurt Pandora, lovely Stesias," Jupiter said.

Pandora awoke. She was now in her right mind.

"What does my love mean?" Pandora asked. "Why does he look so pale and wan?"

"I am pale and wan because of thee, base strumpet," Stesias said.

"Speak mildly to her," Mars said, "or I'll make thee, crabbed, cantankerous swain!"

"Take her again, and love her, Stesias," Sol said.

"Not for Utopia!" Stesias said. "No, not for the world!"

"Ah!" Venus said. "Can thou frown on her who looks so sweet?

"Have I offended thee?" Pandora said. "I'll make amends."

"And what can thou demand more at her hand?" Mercury asked.

"To slay herself, so that I may live alone," Stesias said.

"Flint-hearted shepherd," Luna said, "thou do not deserve her."

Stesias said, "If thou are Jove, convey her from the earth, and punish this Gunophilus: her serving-man."

Gunophilus prayed, "O Jove! Let this be my punishment, to live always with Pandora."

Nature entered the scene. Pandora was her handiwork.

Nature said to the seven planets:

"Envious planets, you have done your worst.

"Yet in despite of you, Pandora lives.

"And because I see that the shepherds have abjured her love, she shall be placed in one of your seven orbs."

An orb is the sphere in which the planet is embedded, according to the geocentric Ptolemaic astronomic theory.

Nature then said to Gunophilus:

"But thou who has not served her as I willed, vanish into a hawthorn as thou stand. Never shall thou wait upon Pandora anymore."

Gunophilus exited, going into a hawthorn bush. He may have metamorphosed and become part of the hawthorn bush.

"O Nature!" Saturn said. "Place Pandora in my sphere, for I am old, and she will make me young."

"Place her with me!" Jupiter said. "And I will leave the Queen of Heaven."

He would leave his wife: Juno.

"Place her with me!" Mars said. "And Venus shall no more be mine."

"Place her with me!" Sol said. "And I'll forget fair Daphne's love."

Phoebus Apollo, the Sun-god, loved the nymph Daphne.

"Place her with me!" Venus said. "And I'll turn Cupid out of doors."

"Place her with me!" Mercury said. "And I'll forsake Aglauros' love."

Hmm. There's an error here. Aglauros was envious of her sister, Herse, whom the god Mercury loved. Aglauros attempted to keep Mercury from seeing Herse, and Mercury turned Aglauros into a stone statue.

Luna said:

"No! Fair Pandora, stay with Cynthia, and I will love thee more than all the rest.

"Rule thou my star, while I stay in the woods, or keep with Pluto in the infernal shades."

Pluto was the god of the Underworld.

Luna is a tripartite goddess. On Earth, she is known as Diana, goddess of the hunt. In the Underworld, she is known as Hecate, goddess of witchcraft. In the Heavens, she is known as Cynthia or as Luna.

"Go wherever thou will as long as I am rid of thee," Stesias said.

"Speak, my Pandora," Nature said. "Where will thou be placed?"

Pandora said:

"Not with old Saturn for he looks like death.

"Nor yet with Jupiter, lest Juno storm.

"Nor with thee, Mars, for Venus is thy love.

"Nor with thee, Sol, for thou have two paramours: the sea-born Thetis and the ruddy Morn.

"Nor with thee, Venus, lest I be in love with blindfolded Cupid or young Joculus.

"Nor with thee, Hermes. Thou are full of slights, and when I need thee, Jove will send thee forth to be his herald.

"Tell me, Cynthia, shall Pandora rule thy star — the Moon — and will thou play Diana in the woods, or Hecate in Pluto's regiment?"

"Aye, Pandora!" Luna said.

Pandora said:

"Fair Nature, let thy handmaid dwell with her because I know that change is my felicity, and fickleness is Pandora's proper form.

"Mercury, thou made me sullen first.

"And thou, Jove, made me proud.

"Thou, Mars, gave me a bloodthirsty mind.

"He — Sol — made me a Puritan.

"Thou, Venus, made me love all whom I saw.

"And thou, Hermes, made me deceive all whom I love.

"But Cynthia made me idle, mutable and changeable, forgetful, foolish, fickle, frantic, mad.

"These are the humors and moods that best content me, and therefore I will stay with Cynthia."

Nature said, "And Stesias, since thou set so light a value on her, be thou her slave, and follow her in the Moon."

"I'll rather die than endure her company!" Stesias said.

"Nature will have it so," Jupiter said. "Attend on her, and be her servant."

"I'll have thee be her vassal," Nature said to Stesias. "Don't murmur and complain."

Stesias said, "Then, to revenge myself on Gunophilus, I'll rend this hawthorn bush with my furious hands, and I'll carry this bush. If ever Pandora looks back, I'll scratch the face of her who was so false to me."

Nature said:

"Now rule, Pandora, in fair Cynthia's place, and make the Moon inconstant like thyself.

"Reign at women's nuptials and weddings, and at their birth.

"Let them be mutable and changeable in all their loves.

"Let them be fantastical, childish, and foolish, in their desires, demanding toys.

"And let them be stark mad when they cannot have their will."

She then said to the seven planets:

"Now follow me, you wandering lights of Heaven, and do not grieve that she is not placed with you.

"All of you shall glance at her in your astronomical aspects, and in astronomical conjunction, all of you shall dwell with her a space."

The planets wander in the sky, and they come closer to and farther away from the Moon as they wander. When they are in astronomical conjunction, they are at their closest to each other.

"I wish that they had my place!" Stesias said.

Nature said, "I order thee to follow her, but do not hurt her."

All exited.

NOTES

— 3.2 —

"Sic vos non vobis; sic vos non vobis."

(3.2.260)

Source of Above:

Lyly, John. *The Woman in the Moon.* Ed. Leah Scragg. The Revels Plays. Manchester and New York: Manchester University Press, 2006. P. 97.

The Latin means: Thus you work not for yourself; thus you work not for yourself.

The poet Virgil wrote *"Sic vos non vobis,"* according to Aelius Donatus' *Life of Virgil,* lamenting that he had worked hard to create lines of poetry, only for another poet to plagiarize them.

Aelius Donatus' *Life of Virgil* is available here:

Donatus, Aelius. *Life of Virgil.* Trans. David Scott Wilson-Okamura. 1996. Rev. 2005, 2008. Online. Internet. 1 January 2023.

www.virgil.org/vitae/a-donatus.htm

Translator: David Wilson-Okamura (1996; rev. 2005, 2008, 2014).

See section 46.

— 5.1 —

I'll wade into the water, water is fair,
And stroke the fishes underneath the gills.
(5.1.29-20)
Source of Above:
Lyly, John. *The Woman in the Moon.* Ed. Leah Scragg. The Revels Plays. Manchester and New York: Manchester University Press, 2006. P. 120.
One method of catching fish is to stroke or tickle the fish under the gills. Wikipedia defines "Trout tickling":

Trout tickling *is the art of rubbing the underbelly of a trout with fingers. If done properly, the trout will go into a trance after a minute or so, and can then easily be retrieved and thrown onto the nearest bit of dry land.*

Source of Above: "Trout tickling." Wikipedia. Accessed 13 June 2022 https://en.wikipedia.org/wiki/Trout_tickling
Wikipedia quotes a 1901 book detailing the practice:

Thomas Martindale's 1901 book, Sport, Indeed, describes the method used on trout in the River Wear in County Durham:

The fish are watched working their way up the shallows and rapids. When they come to the shelter of a ledge or a rock it is their nature to slide under it and rest. The poacher sees the edge of a fin or the moving tail, or maybe he sees neither; instinct, however, tells him a fish ought to be there, so he takes the water very slowly and carefully and stands up near the spot. He then kneels on one knee and passes his hand, turned with fingers up, deftly under the rock until it comes in contact with the fish's tail. Then he begins tickling with his forefinger, gradually running his hand along the fish's belly further and further toward the head until it is under the gills. Then comes a quick grasp, a struggle, and the prize is wrenched out of his natural element, stunned with a blow on the head, and landed in the pocket of the poacher.

Source of Above: "Trout tickling." Wikipedia. Accessed 13 June 2022
https://en.wikipedia.org/wiki/Trout_tickling
Look up "Trout Tickling" on YouTube. Here is one video:

Trout Tickling on the Elk River (YouTube)

Is trout tickling real? Has it ever really been done? Watch the video taken on the Elk River near Fernie BC in September 2008 and you decide!

https://www.youtube.com/watch?v=tszDNiPqm5c&t=66s

— 5.1 —

O Marce fili, annum iam audientem Cratip-
    pum, idque Athenis."
(5.1.123-24)
Source of Above:
Lyly, John. *The Woman in the Moon.* Ed. Leah Scragg. The Revels Plays. Manchester and New York: Manchester University Press, 2006. P. 124.

The Latin is the beginning of Cicero's *De Officiis.*

The source of the quotation I used is this:

Loeb Classical Library, Harvard University Press, vol. XXI, 1913; Latin text with facing English translation by Walter Miller. It is in the public domain.

http://penelope.uchicago.edu/Thayer/E/Roman/Texts/Cicero/de_Officiis/home.html

https://penelope.uchicago.edu/Thayer/E/Roman/Texts/Cicero/de_Officiis/1A*.html

— Entire Play —

Nature is a merciful god.

Early in the play, Nature tells the seven planets, "If thus you cross the meed of my deserts — resist giving me what I deserve — and interfere with what I have created, be sure that I will dissolve your harmony, when once you touch the fixed period of your sway."

The seven planets do indeed interfere with what Nature has created by giving Pandora different personality traits, but Nature does not change their harmony into disharmony. All she does is make Pandora the Woman in the Moon.

APPENDIX A: FAIR USE

§ 107. Limitations on exclusive rights: Fair use

Release date: 2004-04-30

Notwithstanding the provisions of sections 106 and 106A, the fair use of a copyrighted work, including such use by reproduction in copies or phonorecords or by any other means specified by that section, for purposes such as criticism, comment, news reporting, teaching (including multiple copies for classroom use), scholarship, or research, is not an infringement of copyright. In determining whether the use made of a work in any particular case is a fair use the factors to be considered shall include —

(1) the purpose and character of the use, including whether such use is of a commercial nature or is for nonprofit educational purposes;

(2) the nature of the copyrighted work;

(3) the amount and substantiality of the portion used in relation to the copyrighted work as a whole; and

(4) the effect of the use upon the potential market for or value of the copyrighted work.

The fact that a work is unpublished shall not itself bar a finding of fair use if such finding is made upon consideration of all the above factors.

Source of Fair Use information:

http://www.law.cornell.edu/uscode/17/107.html

APPENDIX B: ABOUT THE AUTHOR

It was a dark and stormy night. Suddenly a cry rang out, and on a hot summer night in 1954, Josephine, wife of Carl Bruce, gave birth to a boy — me. Unfortunately, this young married couple allowed Reuben Saturday, Josephine's brother, to name their first-born. Reuben, aka "The Joker," decided that Bruce was a nice name, so he decided to name me Bruce Bruce. I have gone by my middle name — David — ever since.

Being named Bruce David Bruce hasn't been all bad. Bank tellers remember me very quickly, so I don't often have to show an ID. It can be fun in charades, also. When I was a counselor as a teenager at Camp Echoing Hills in Warsaw, Ohio, a fellow counselor gave the signs for "sounds like" and "two words," then she pointed to a bruise on her leg twice. Bruise Bruise? Oh yeah, Bruce Bruce is the answer!

Uncle Reuben, by the way, gave me a haircut when I was in kindergarten. He cut my hair short and shaved a small bald spot on the back of my head. My mother wouldn't let me go to school until the bald spot grew out again.

Of all my brothers and sisters (six in all), I am the only transplant to Athens, Ohio. I was born in Newark, Ohio, and have lived all around Southeastern Ohio. However, I moved to Athens to go to Ohio University and have never left.

At Ohio U, I never could make up my mind whether to major in English or Philosophy, so I got a bachelor's degree with a double major in both areas, then I added a Master of Arts degree in English and a Master of Arts degree in Philosophy. Yes, I have my MAMA degree.

Currently, and for a long time to come (I eat fruits and veggies), I am spending my retirement writing books such as *Nadia Comaneci: Perfect 10*, *The Funniest People in Comedy*, *Homer's* Iliad: *A Retelling in Prose*, and *William Shakespeare's* Hamlet: *A Retelling in Prose*.

If all goes well, I will publish one or two books a year for the rest of my life. (On the other hand, a good way to make God laugh is to tell Her your plans.)

By the way, my sister Brenda Kennedy writes romances such as *A New Beginning* and *Shattered Dreams*.

APPENDIX C: SOME BOOKS BY DAVID BRUCE

Retellings of a Classic Work of Literature

Arden of Faversham: A Retelling

Ben Jonson's The Alchemist: *A Retelling*

Ben Jonson's The Arraignment, or Poetaster: *A Retelling*

Ben Jonson's Bartholomew Fair: *A Retelling*

Ben Jonson's The Case is Altered: *A Retelling*

Ben Jonson's Catiline's Conspiracy: *A Retelling*

Ben Jonson's The Devil is an Ass: *A Retelling*

Ben Jonson's Epicene: *A Retelling*

Ben Jonson's Every Man in His Humor: *A Retelling*

Ben Jonson's Every Man Out of His Humor: *A Retelling*

Ben Jonson's The Fountain of Self-Love, or Cynthia's Revels: *A Retelling*

Ben Jonson's The Magnetic Lady, or Humors Reconciled: *A Retelling*

Ben Jonson's The New Inn, or The Light Heart: *A Retelling*

Ben Jonson's Sejanus' Fall: *A Retelling*

Ben Jonson's The Staple of News: *A Retelling*

Ben Jonson's A Tale of a Tub: *A Retelling*

Ben Jonson's Volpone, or the Fox: *A Retelling*

Christopher Marlowe's Complete Plays: Retellings

Christopher Marlowe's Dido, Queen of Carthage: *A Retelling*

Christopher Marlowe's Doctor Faustus: *Retellings of the 1604 A-Text and of the 1616 B-Text*

Christopher Marlowe's Edward II: *A Retelling*

Christopher Marlowe's The Massacre at Paris: *A Retelling*

Christopher Marlowe's The Rich Jew of Malta: *A Retelling*

Christopher Marlowe's Tamburlaine, Parts 1 and 2: *Retellings*

Dante's Divine Comedy: *A Retelling in Prose*

Dante's Inferno: *A Retelling in Prose*

Dante's Purgatory: *A Retelling in Prose*

Dante's Paradise: *A Retelling in Prose*

The Famous Victories of Henry V: A Retelling

From the Iliad *to the* Odyssey: *A Retelling in Prose of Quintus of Smyrna's* Posthomerica

George Chapman, Ben Jonson, and John Marston's Eastward Ho! *A Retelling*

George Peele's The Arraignment of Paris: *A Retelling*

George Peele's The Battle of Alcazar: *A Retelling*

George Peele's David and Bathsheba, and the Tragedy of Absalom: *A Retelling*

George Peele's Edward I: *A Retelling*

George Peele's The Old Wives' Tale: *A Retelling*

George-a-Greene: *A Retelling*

The History of King Leir: *A Retelling*

Homer's Iliad: *A Retelling in Prose*

Homer's Odyssey: *A Retelling in Prose*

J.W. Gent.'s The Valiant Scot: *A Retelling*

Jason and the Argonauts: A Retelling in Prose of Apollonius of Rhodes' Argonautica

John Ford: Eight Plays Translated into Modern English

John Ford's The Broken Heart: *A Retelling*

John Ford's The Fancies, Chaste and Noble: *A Retelling*

John Ford's The Lady's Trial: *A Retelling*

John Ford's The Lover's Melancholy: *A Retelling*

John Ford's Love's Sacrifice: *A Retelling*

John Ford's Perkin Warbeck: *A Retelling*

John Ford's The Queen: *A Retelling*

John Ford's 'Tis Pity She's a Whore: *A Retelling*

John Lyly's Campaspe: *A Retelling*

John Lyly's Endymion, The Man in the Moon: *A Retelling*

John Lyly's Galatea: *A Retelling*

John Lyly's Love's Metamorphosis: *A Retelling*

John Lyly's Midas: *A Retelling*

John Lyly's Mother Bombie: *A Retelling*

John Lyly's Sappho and Phao: *A Retelling*

John Lyly's The Woman in the Moon: *A Retelling*

John Webster's The White Devil: *A Retelling*

King Edward III: *A Retelling*

Mankind: *A Medieval Morality Play* (A Retelling)

Margaret Cavendish's The Unnatural Tragedy: *A Retelling*

The Merry Devil of Edmonton: *A Retelling*

The Summoning of Everyman: *A Medieval Morality Play* (A Retelling)

Robert Greene's Friar Bacon and Friar Bungay: *A Retelling*

The Taming of a Shrew: *A Retelling*

Tarlton's Jests: A Retelling

Thomas Middleton's A Chaste Maid in Cheapside: *A Retelling*

Thomas Middleton's Women Beware Women: *A Retelling*

Thomas Middleton and Thomas Dekker's The Roaring Girl: *A Retelling*

Thomas Middleton and William Rowley's The Changeling: *A Retelling*

The Trojan War and Its Aftermath: Four Ancient Epic Poems

Virgil's Aeneid: *A Retelling in Prose*

William Shakespeare's 5 Late Romances: Retellings in Prose

William Shakespeare's 10 Histories: Retellings in Prose

William Shakespeare's 11 Tragedies: Retellings in Prose

William Shakespeare's 12 Comedies: Retellings in Prose

William Shakespeare's 38 Plays: Retellings in Prose
William Shakespeare's 1 Henry IV, aka Henry IV, Part 1: A Retelling in Prose
William Shakespeare's 2 Henry IV, aka Henry IV, Part 2: A Retelling in Prose
William Shakespeare's 1 Henry VI, aka Henry VI, Part 1: A Retelling in Prose
William Shakespeare's 2 Henry VI, aka Henry VI, Part 2: A Retelling in Prose
William Shakespeare's 3 Henry VI, aka Henry VI, Part 3: A Retelling in Prose
William Shakespeare's All's Well that Ends Well: A Retelling in Prose
William Shakespeare's Antony and Cleopatra: A Retelling in Prose
William Shakespeare's As You Like It: A Retelling in Prose
William Shakespeare's The Comedy of Errors: A Retelling in Prose
William Shakespeare's Coriolanus: A Retelling in Prose
William Shakespeare's Cymbeline: A Retelling in Prose
William Shakespeare's Hamlet: A Retelling in Prose
William Shakespeare's Henry V: A Retelling in Prose
William Shakespeare's Henry VIII: A Retelling in Prose
William Shakespeare's Julius Caesar: A Retelling in Prose
William Shakespeare's King John: A Retelling in Prose
William Shakespeare's King Lear: A Retelling in Prose
William Shakespeare's Love's Labor's Lost: A Retelling in Prose
William Shakespeare's Macbeth: A Retelling in Prose
William Shakespeare's Measure for Measure: A Retelling in Prose
William Shakespeare's The Merchant of Venice: A Retelling in Prose
William Shakespeare's The Merry Wives of Windsor: A Retelling in Prose
William Shakespeare's A Midsummer Night's Dream: A Retelling in Prose
William Shakespeare's Much Ado About Nothing: A Retelling in Prose
William Shakespeare's Othello: A Retelling in Prose
William Shakespeare's Pericles, Prince of Tyre: A Retelling in Prose
William Shakespeare's Richard II: A Retelling in Prose
William Shakespeare's Richard III: A Retelling in Prose
William Shakespeare's Romeo and Juliet: A Retelling in Prose
William Shakespeare's The Taming of the Shrew: A Retelling in Prose
William Shakespeare's The Tempest: A Retelling in Prose
William Shakespeare's Timon of Athens: A Retelling in Prose
William Shakespeare's Titus Andronicus: A Retelling in Prose
William Shakespeare's Troilus and Cressida: A Retelling in Prose
William Shakespeare's Twelfth Night: A Retelling in Prose
William Shakespeare's The Two Gentlemen of Verona: A Retelling in Prose
William Shakespeare's The Two Noble Kinsmen: A Retelling in Prose
William Shakespeare's The Winter's Tale: A Retelling in Prose